"A solid choice for traditional mystery fans, *Murder in the Raw* provides some new twists on something old and familiar."

—*Mystery Reader*

"*Murder in the Raw* is one of the more recent contributions to a growing library of mystery novels of interest to naturists, and naked readers will especially enjoy how Challinor 'gets it right.'"

—*N: Nude and Natural*

Christmas Is Murder

"[A] winner ... At times, it seems we are playing Clue or perhaps enjoying a contemporary retelling of a classic Agatha Christie tale (*And Then There Were None*, or *At Bertram's Hotel*) with a charming new sleuth. A must for cozy fans."   —*Booklist* (starred review)

"Challinor's debut is a pleasant modern knockoff of Christie."

—*Kirkus Reviews*

"Graves's next case may be worth watching for."

—*Ellery Queen Mystery Magazine*

"Challinor will keep most readers guessing as she cleverly spreads suspicion and clues that point in one direction, then another."

—*Alfred Hitchcock Mystery Magazine*

"Shades of Agatha Christie and all that. You may not even want to save this one for the holidays."   —BookBitch.com

"A great start to a new series that is sure to become a modern favorite traditional English cozy series."   —The Mystery Reader

"Agatha Christie fans, here you go! You have been waiting for a mystery writer that can hold the torch, well we found her: C.S. Challinor."

—*Suspense Magazine*

"*Christmas is Murder* is a most enjoyable first mystery in what promises to be a fantastic series. Challinor writes with wit and cheek, and with Rex Graves, she has created a thoroughly charming sleuth."

—Rick Miller, author of *Bigger Than Jesus*
and host of ABC's primetime hit series "Just for Laughs"

"C.S. Challinor has crafted a delectable murder mystery set in an old English manor turned hotel. *Christmas is Murder* has all the charm and ambience of a classic Agatha Christie novel. This is mystery at its very best! Challinor is an author to watch. I'll be anxiously awaiting her next book!"

—Nancy Mehl, author of The Ivy Towers Mystery Series

"Eat some shortbread, make a cup of tea, and curl up with a good book."

—Barbara Selvaggio, Walkers Shortbread US

MURDER

— comes —

CALLING

ALSO BY C. S. CHALLINOR

Christmas is Murder
Murder in the Raw
Phi Beta Murder
Murder on the Moor
Murder of the Bride
Murder at Midnight

A Rex Graves Mystery

MURDER

⌐ comes ⌐

CALLING

C. S. CHALLINOR

MIDNIGHT INK
WOODBURY, MINNESOTA

First Edition
First Printing, 2015

Book design by Donna Burch-Brown
Cover design by Kevin R. Brown
Cover illustration by iStockphoto.com/35821812/©Sylphe_7
            iStockphoto.com/17843044/©GeorgHanf
Editing by Kathy Schneider

Midnight Ink, an imprint of Llewellyn Worldwide Ltd.

Library of Congress Cataloging-in-Publication Data

Challinor, C. S. (Caroline S.)
  Murder comes calling / C.S. Challinor. — First edition.
     pages ;   cm. — (A Rex Graves mystery ; #7)
  ISBN 978-0-7387-4548-0
1. Graves, Rex (Fictitious character)—Fiction. 2.
Murder—Investigation—Fiction. I. Title.
  PS3603.H3366M86 2015
  813'.6—dc23
                                                    2014045139

Midnight Ink
Llewellyn Worldwide Ltd.
2143 Wooddale Drive
Woodbury, MN 55125-2989
www.midnightinkbooks.com

Printed in the United States of America

DEDICATION

To fellow travellers and beautiful friends,
Patty and Abe, from Texas.

ACKNOWLEDGMENTS

Grateful thanks once again to "Mom" Neillie Miller for reading my manuscripts before they go to the editor.

ONE

"IMAGINE——MURDERED IN YOUR OWN home!" Mrs. Graves shook her snowy head. "Three homes in one day, and all in the same neighbourhood! Soon we'll have to keep guns, like in America." She set the *Scotsman* down on the breakfast table. "The story describes Notting Hamlet as a quiet residential community. Doesn't your friend Malcolm live there?"

Malcolm Patterson had moved to Bedfordshire after graduating from Edinburgh University at the same time as her son.

"He does," Rex said guardedly. When the subject of murder came up in the media, his mother invariably enquired if he would be involved in the case, thinking he spent enough time dealing with heinous crimes in his day job at the High Court of Justiciary. "He became a pathologist," he added in a conversational tone.

"Nice lad, Malcolm. Morbid profession."

"Not a lad anymore," Rex pointed out, wondering if he should forego the extra toast in his on-going effort to curb excess weight on his midsection.

"And such grisly murders," his mother went on, picking up the paper again. She peered at him over her spectacles. "I don't suppose ...," she began.

Rex knew what was coming. The decision regarding the toast was made. "Got to hurry," he said, casting aside his linen napkin. "I have to be in court."

"Who are you prosecuting?"

"An arsonist."

"I hope no one died in the fire," she declared. "Such a horrible way to go!"

On his way into the hall, Rex ran into Miss Bird, the elderly housekeeper. "Mother is in one of her maudlin moods," he warned.

"Did somebody die?" Miss Bird asked with alarm. Such an occurrence was common among people of their acquaintance, most of whom were getting on in years.

"Four people in a riverfront community in England." Rex pulled on his raincoat and grabbed his brolly from the stand. "You'll hear aboot it in the news—if you don't hear aboot it from Mother first."

"Was it the flu?"

"No. A serial killer."

Miss Bird gasped.

"Make sure you lock the front door behind you," his mother called from the parlour. Still possessed of the hearing of a bat, she missed little of what went on around her.

"I'll lock after ye," the housekeeper assured Rex as he opened the door to a blast of cold air and confronted the terraced street of respectable Victorian grey stone homes, bleak beneath the drizzling rain.

His fiancée was at that moment on her way to Aruba with her friend Julie, having failed to entice him to join her, even though she knew how he felt about cruises. All those sunburned hordes rampaging over the ship in search of fun and food, Rex thought with mild distaste as his polished leather shoe proceeded to sink into an icy puddle, soaking his sock. For a brief second he almost regretted forfeiting the cruise. But no, he decided it was just as well. Malcolm had called him from Notting Hamlet the previous evening. As Rex's mother had feared, her son was soon to be immersed in his favourite hobby of murder.

TWO

On a gloomy afternoon towards the end of November, Rex drove south along the A1 past the A421 junction to Bedford and continued another six miles before exiting the motorway and heading east. He had memorized the directions to Notting Hamlet and still managed to miss a turn on the lonely country roads, which was uncharacteristic of him, since he prided himself on his navigational skills. This, after the long drive from Edinburgh, much of it in the rain, contrived to put him in a rare bad mood.

When he finally arrived at Malcolm Patterson's address, tired and irritated, his friend took one look at him upon opening the front door and declared, "You got lost."

"How did you guess?"

"Don't let it get to you," Malcolm said, closing the door behind them. "Everyone does. It's the ruddy signposts. Or, rather, the lack of them." He took Rex's dripping brolly that had shielded his guest from car to house.

"It's as if you lot do not want to be found," Rex said, less gruffly, giving his friend a warm handshake.

Malcolm laughed. "You may be right. We're a bit off the beaten track out here." Originally from Edinburgh, he still retained the shortened vowels and slight aspiration on the "w" that characterized Rex's speech, though his "out" was pronounced less as an "oot."

"But it seems someone managed to find us," he added with a grim smile.

Rex's spirits lifted. After all, that was why he had come: To find out who had murdered four of Notting Hamlet's long-time residents.

"Well, come on through and warm yourself by the fire," Malcolm invited, leading Rex into a living room at the back of the house.

The room exhibited a woman's touch, floral and cosy. A handwoven hearthrug lay in front of the flint stone fireplace, which had been converted to gas. Clearly, Malcolm had not changed the decor since his wife passed away three years ago. He had taken her sudden death hard and had quit his job at the mortuary.

Rex sat down in the recliner indicated by his friend and felt the strain of the long journey ebb away, along with the stiffness in his lower back. "Do you know what today is?" he asked Malcolm.

"Is it an anniversary?"

"It's Thanksgiving in America. On the fourth Thursday of November they give thanks and cook a turkey, pretty much like we do at Christmas."

"So what do they do for Christmas?"

"I think they cook a ham."

"Well, there's no ham or turkey for dinner, I'm afraid. Tea or Scotch for now?" Malcolm offered.

"Tea would be grand."

While his host went off to fulfil his request, Rex sat back and closed his eyes, the warmth from the gas fire enveloping him and making him feel suddenly sleepy. The sounds of a ratting tea tray woke him just as he was nodding off into a light slumber.

"Age will do that to you," his friend said.

"Do what?" Rex sat up in his recliner, blinking.

"Make one doze off in front of the fire."

"Speak for yourself. I just drove all the way from Edinburgh, remember."

"Aye, well," Malcolm conceded. "And most of the way in the rain, no doubt. It hasn't stopped all week here." He poured out the tea. "Is it still three lumps of sugar?"

"It is."

Rex waited for his doctor friend to make some remark about health and diet, but none was forthcoming. He hadn't seen Malcolm since his wife's funeral. Rex had been shocked at the time to find him turned grey from grief. They had kept loosely in touch by phone and through cards at Christmas until the urgent call regarding the murders. Rex had felt it was the least he could do to travel to south-central England and offer his old college friend what assistance he could, if only moral support. He worried Malcolm might have a relapse under the strain of dealing with more death right on his doorstep, so to speak.

The riverfront community of Notting Hamlet was small, containing seventy homes, and most of the residents were acquainted to one extent or the other. Malcolm had intimated on the phone that he had been on neighbourly terms with the victims, and was distressed by the grim circumstances of their respective demises, each killed in a different manner. Rex asked his old friend to bring him up to date with developments in the case.

Malcolm sat down, cup of tea in hand. "The police haven't released many details. But due to the nature of the murders, they've cautioned us to keep our doors and windows locked and to install burglar alarms. That's all nonsense, of course, since the victims obviously knew the killer. In none of the cases were there signs of forced entry."

"The victims didn't need to have known the killer," Rex countered. "They could have answered the door to a stranger."

"Possibly, but the front doors are all equipped with peepholes," Malcolm informed him. "Same builder for all the homes. I'll show you around in the morning. There are four different floor plans, but the level of finish is much the same in all. Good quality materials and similar landscaping to give Notting Hamlet a nice uniform look and feel."

From what Rex had already seen, the houses ranged from villas to two-storey homes with half-timbered tan stucco façades and small-paned windows. Squat chimneys rose from the steep, brown-tiled roofs. Rex felt sure the developer would have stipulated thatch, had it been practical. It seemed he or she had strived for a rustic look for the community, the setting enhanced by a strategic spattering of mature trees.

"It's an older community," Malcolm went on, almost apologetically, "but well established and quiet. No new construction or so-called 'improvements' that you find in other developments."

"No plans to move, I take it, in spite of the recent murders?" Rex asked.

"I'm settled here. And I feel Jocelyn's presence around me, which I find comforting. A couple of ladies—single ladies, I might add—" Malcolm said with a blush, "have told me it's time to move on. But I have my routine, and I'd rather not go through a major life change at the moment, not when I'm finally coming to terms with my wife's death."

"I understand," Rex said, although he had at times thought Malcolm rather lacking in motivation. His friend had every right to live as he chose, after all. As far as Rex knew, he was living off the money from a life insurance policy taken out on his wife when they were first married fifteen years ago. He had no children to answer to, and his parents were dead. Rex glanced at his pensive friend across the coffee table. Poor Malcolm was very much alone in this world.

"Well, if you ever decide to return to Scotland, let me know. A visit would be grand. My mother's place has several spare bedrooms, if you recall, and you haven't seen my lodge in the Highlands yet. You'd enjoy the wildlife and scenery."

"Most kind," Malcolm murmured non-committedly. "It's so long since I've been back home."

"I know. You're beginning to lose the accent. You sound more like a Sassenach now."

Malcolm nodded and smiled. "Look, I'm not much of a cook, as you know, but I have some frozen dinners from Marks & Spencer. Will that do you?"

"Is there no pub around here where we can get some grub?"

"Not for seven miles of winding back roads, and it's sloshing down rain."

"Frozen will be fine," Rex conceded.

"Won't be a sec." Malcolm got up from his armchair. "Switch on the news, if you like. I thought we could eat in here by the fire. It's what I usually do—use one of those TV tables." He indicated two identical items of furniture with Z-shaped legs designed to slot over one's lap as he left the living room.

Rex would have preferred to go out to eat, but he felt better when his friend returned with a glass tankard of Guinness.

"I stocked up on your favourite tipple."

"Most kind."

"Oh, that's the microwave beeping. Dinner will be right up." Malcolm hurried away again and Rex grabbed the remote for the six o'clock news. An eager young male reporter in a windbreaker stood by the sign at the stone-pillared entrance to Notting Hamlet and announced that a man was helping the police with their inquiries into the killing of Ernest Blackwell, 81; Valerie Trotter, 47; Barry Burns, 79; and Vic Chandler, 55. As rain trickled down his hood, the reporter reiterated the brutal nature of the crimes and deplored how such a thing could have happened in this sleepy little community.

Generally, the police did not advertise the fact they had a person of interest unless they were almost sure they had the right person, Rex mused.

"No mention of the suspect's name yet," Malcolm said, returning with a bowl of cheese puffs. "But rumour has it it's the house agent I told you about on the phone. Chris Walker. I still think it's a fit-up. I mean, Walker isn't the brightest bulb on the tree, but you'd think he would have covered his tracks better if he really was the murderer."

"I wonder what could have been his motive."

"The police don't need motive, do they? Not when there's piles of evidence. For all we know, he could be a psychopath."

"You're the doctor, Malcolm. Does this Chris Walker seem like a psychopath to you?"

"I'm a pathologist, not a psychiatrist. All I can tell you is it's often hard to know for certain. Especially with sociopaths. Walker fits that mould all right. Personable, smooth. Perhaps a little too smooth. But most salespeople are like that. And he can be a bit pushy and has got a few people's backs up. Oh, our meals. Almost forgot. Be right back."

While Malcolm went to fetch dinner, Rex considered what could have made the police hone in on the house agent: Probably the fact the four victims each had their home up for sale, all listed through Chris Walker. Malcolm had told Rex about this bizarre coincidence during their first phone conversation. But three other homes were up for sale in Notting Hamlet, and their owners weren't dead—yet.

THREE

Malcolm returned with the dinners in their containers, served on china plates. "Fish and chips pie, one of my new faves. Hope you like it."

"Thank you."

"And another Guinness." He handed Rex the black can with the trademark gold harp and seated himself in the other recliner. He took up the remote and the burble on the TV ceased, leaving the patter of rain on the darkened panes to fill the void.

You couldn't beat Marks & Spencer's supermarket chain for ready-made meals, Rex thought, tasting the pie. Not everyone had the luxury of a cook-housekeeper like Miss Bird. "So, if Walker is not our man," he continued, "how do you propose we proceed?" He opened the can and refilled his glass.

His friend took a moment to answer while he finished chewing a mouthful of food, then dabbed at his lips with a napkin. "Not saying categorically it *isn't* him, just that the police might be jumping the gun and we shouldn't postpone our own investigation. Besides,"

Malcolm added with an air of mystery, "we may be apprised of a clue the police are not in possession of yet."

"Ah." Rex, in turn, wiped his mouth and the top of his beard with his napkin. So Malcolm had not brought him to Bedfordshire on a completely wild goose chase. He breathed a sigh of relief. There was nothing more irksome than walking away from an unresolved case, especially when he had asked his law clerk to rearrange his schedule to accommodate his friend, who had made a heartfelt plea for his assistance. "Well, let's have it," he said.

Malcolm pushed his half-eaten pie aside and turned in his recliner to fully face Rex. "First, I must ask you to listen through to the end without judging."

Rex stared back at him. "Go on," he said cautiously.

"I hope you'll understand why I did what I did. But if I get into trouble for withholding information from the police, I trust you will lend me your best legal advice. I know," Malcolm pre-empted, holding up his palm. "You practice Scottish law, and this is England, but it works much the same way, as does police procedure."

"Malcolm," Rex said with emphasis, "did you invite me down here to help solve this case or do you need me to help get you oot of trouble?"

"I hope the latter won't be necessary. Perhaps if I just explain, you can help me sort it out?"

Oh dear, thought Rex, beginning to regret his trip. Couldn't Malcolm have just sought his advice on the phone? He dropped his napkin on the tray and invited his friend to explain.

"Well, it's like this," Malcolm began. "Lottie Green, who lives next door to Ernest Blackwell on Fox Lane—he's the oldest of the four victims—well, she found him first. Dead, I mean. She was fetching her cat, which had strayed into his back garden, and noticed a pair of feet sticking out from under the piano."

"In other words, she looked through the window," Rex inserted.

"Well, yes. Lottie is a bit nosy. But she means well," Malcolm hastened to add. "She cleans for me on occasion and is perfectly reliable. Anyway, thinking he'd had a heart attack, she ran back to her house and called me, because I'm a medical practitioner." He gave a modest cough.

He had not practiced medicine in three years, Rex refrained from pointing out, and instead asked the obvious question: Why hadn't she called for an ambulance?

"Ernest had a fear of hospitals. Everyone knew that. And I was on hand."

"So, what happened next?" Rex asked with mounting curiosity. Hitherto, Malcolm had only supplied him with the briefest of details concerning the case. The rest he had gleaned from the papers. "Were you the first person to see the entire body and what really happened to him?"

"Yes, and just as well. It was a gory scene, I can tell you. His head had all but been severed from his body. If Lottie had found him in that state, she would have been the one to go into cardiac arrest, I'm sure."

"Ernest Blackwell was the victim garrotted with piano wire," Rex confirmed, recalling what he had read in the papers.

"Right, almost to his spine."

"You didn't tell me you were first on the scene," Rex said.

"Ah, well, here comes the difficult part. First I should explain that I came in the front door, which wasn't locked, as I informed the police when they arrived. Naturally, I called nine-nine-nine when

I found Mr. Blackwell in that state, which is to say obviously murdered."

"Obviously?"

"If you slit your own throat to that extent, you are in no fit state to chuck the piano wire across the room, believe me. And there was no blood between that and the body, so he couldn't have stumbled to the piano."

"Hm," Rex said. "No attempt to conceal the weapon or that it was, apparently, a murder."

"Indeed. Quite brazen. And there's more."

Rex waited while Malcolm made a visible effort to prepare himself for what he had to say. He straightened in his recliner, looked at Rex, and sighed. Exercising the utmost patience, Rex gazed back and waited. "Och, spit it oot, man," he finally spluttered in exasperation.

"Right, then. Well, nor do decapitated persons smear letters on their forehead in their own blood. Not to my knowledge, anyway. Unless Ernest drew blood first, wrote the letters, and then made the final cut and somehow landed on the other side of the room."

"I don't remember reading anything concerning letters written in blood on the victim's forehead."

Malcolm scratched behind his ear. "Well, you wouldn't. I wiped them off before anyone could see them.

"You did what?" Rex exploded. "What were you thinking?"

"I was thinking if I didn't get rid of those letters, I would be incriminated."

"How do you mean? What did the letters say?"

"M-N-P In capitals."

"Those are your initials!"

"Don't I know it. Now can you see my predicament?"

Rex stared in shock at his friend. "Notwithstanding, you of all people should know better. You've worked with detectives, examining bodies to determine cause of death and whether foul play was involved."

"That's true. And I also know how detectives operate. If I'd left my initials on the body, it would only have been a matter of time before I turned from witness to suspect. And it would have been a waste of police time since I didn't do it!"

"Malcolm." Rex took a deep breath. "It's a vital piece of evidence. Once the police cleared you—if you had come under suspicion— they could have followed other leads. Such a big potential clue could serve to nail the house agent or else exonerate him. You must tell the police immediately before the wrong individual is put behind bars. The longer you wait, the worse it will be for you."

"I'd get prison time for tampering with evidence. I could even lose my medical license."

"Pity you didn't think of that before. And while I sit here doing nothing aboot it, I'm aiding and abetting. Did you consider how your ill-conceived action might affect me, and what an awkward position you might be placing me in?" Rex could feel his face turning beetroot. His fiancée said when he got really angry, his face turned redder than his hair. He took a large gulp of Guinness.

"I know, Rex. It was stupid. I panicked."

"But if you had nothing to hide, why risk it?"

"It's a small community. I couldn't bear the thought of everyone viewing me with suspicion even if the murderer was caught. You have no idea what people are like around here. Everybody knows everybody's business. They have nothing better to do than gossip and perpetuate feuds."

Rex pushed his TV table away and let his head drop into his hands. "Oh, Malcolm," he said in a muffled voice. After a moment's thought, he pulled himself together. "Let's drive down to the station this minute, get it all sorted. I'll explain you were under severe stress and made a mistake on the spur of the moment."

"That might fly if it was just the one instance," Malcolm mumbled, gazing at his hands in his lap. "But, you see, the same letters were scrawled over the other victims' foreheads as well."

"And you ..."

"Yes, I wiped all of them clean."

When Rex had recovered sufficiently from the extent of Malcolm's confession, several questions came flooding into his mind. "And Lottie didn't see what was written on Ernest Blackwell's forehead?"

"No. She followed me into his house through the front door, but when I saw the pool of blood by the piano I told her to stay outside the room and call the police. And then I closed the door."

"Did you touch anything else?"

"No, I didn't even need to check for a pulse. I mean, his throat ... well, it was split in two."

Rex shivered even though Malcolm's living room was beginning to feel uncomfortably warm. He divested himself of his tweed jacket. "And the others?"

"After seeing there was nothing to be done for the old man, I left the room and went to find Lottie. She wasn't in the house, but I noticed the table in the kitchen was set for two. Ernest lived on his own. Worried there might be another victim, I ended up searching the garage. And that's where I found Valerie Trotter, dead from carbon monoxide poisoning inside Ernest's old Daimler. I pulled her out and opened the garage door to let in fresh air, but she was past reviving. I left the engine running with the hose in the exhaust for the police to deal with."

Well, that's something, Rex thought with irony. "And at some point you wiped off the letters on her forehead."

"Yes," Malcolm admitted. "But I tried to resuscitate her first."

"Were the letters written in blood?"

"Presumably Ernest's blood. There was no other blood on her."

"But we'll never know for certain that it was Ernest's blood, will we? Because now it can never be tested."

"I know, Rex. Please don't rub it in. But don't you see? Having got rid of the letters on Ernest, I had to do the same with Valerie."

Rex merely raised an eyebrow in response. "The papers said the bodies had not been dead long?"

"No, they were not yet in rigor. The blood on the sitting room carpet wasn't even fully dry."

"So Valerie was found at Ernie's house," Rex ruminated aloud. "She could have been collateral damage. What was the connection between her and Ernest?"

"No idea. But, as I said, the table was set for two, the plates clean. I got there about three. She might have been the lunch guest."

"She was forty-seven, correct? And Ernest was in his early eighties. Unlikely there was anything romantic going on between them."

"Granted, Valerie was no spring chicken, but she was still a looker in a tarty sort of way. And Ernest had a way with him that seemed to appeal to the ladies. He was still spry, was old Ernie, though he complained of arthritis."

"He went by Ernie?" Rex enquired, so caught up in the case by now that he managed to relegate his friend's unconscionable acts to the back of his mind while he processed the new information.

"I shouldn't have said Ernie," Malcolm corrected himself. "He couldn't abide being called that. But he was more of an Ernie than an Ernest, if you know what I mean. He was very gabby, although sometimes he would just clam up," his friend added in a reflective tone. "Onset of Alzheimer's, perhaps. It could be he just forgot things. At his age, that's entirely possible."

"Well, you had better tell me aboot the other two," Rex said in a resigned tone. Intentionally and systematically destroying evidence could never be construed as being other than premeditated. How Malcolm expected him to get him out of this predicament was yet another mystery.

"Barry Burns and Vic Chandler," Malcolm began after a hasty sip of water. "They lived here on Badger Court almost opposite each other. Their properties were up for sale, too. Well, after I located Lottie and told her that Valerie Trotter was also dead, I asked her to stay outside Ernest's house and wait for the police. I needed to dispose of my handkerchief."

"Because it had blood on it," Rex remarked dryly.

"Correct. So I went home and soaked it in bleach and cold water."

This only gets worse, Rex thought, his stomach tightening in anguish as he waited to hear what else his friend had to say.

FOUR

"WOULD YOU CARE FOR some coffee?" Malcolm asked Rex. "I know I could do with some."

"Aye, it looks like it's going to be a long night." They were only halfway through the confession.

Presumably, Malcolm would justify his cover-up on the other two bodies in the same way, by saying he was only trying to protect himself. But how had he discovered them before anyone else did? Rex began to feel rather uneasy as he helped Malcolm clear their tables. He followed his friend into the kitchen—better to keep an eye on him. A whole new dimension to Malcolm's character was beginning to emerge. Rex had always known him to be a careful and steady sort of soul, certainly not one to give into criminal impulses, even when his freedom might be in jeopardy.

Surely no one would believe the mild-mannered doctor to be a murderer, in spite of his initials being coincidentally or deliberately emblazoned on the victims' bodies. And yet who could have thought him capable of tampering with evidence, especially in a murder case? And not just once, but four times? Rex had an especially hard time getting his head around that. He would hear his friend out and then insist they go to the police. After all, an innocent man could be going to prison for life based on incomplete facts. Oh, what a mess, he lamented.

Malcolm loaded the few plates and utensils into the dishwasher and then busied himself with the coffee maker while Rex rinsed out the glasses. The appliances had obviously not been updated since the nineties when the development had been built.

When the coffee was ready, they moved back to the living room. Rex adjusted his recliner so he could converse more easily with Malcolm and hear the rest of his astounding account. "So, I'm assuming you must have found the other two bodies before the police arrived. How did that happen?"

"Lottie had tried to call Barry, Ernest's golfing friend, to give him the sad news, but he wasn't answering his phone. So I said I would swing by, since he lived close to me and, anyway, I needed an excuse to hurry off and do something about the handkerchief."

Rex gave an eloquently disapproving cough, but said nothing.

Malcolm quickly continued his story. "I rang and knocked at Barry's door, but there was no answer. I found the door unlocked, like at Ernest's, and walked right in. Well, I didn't have to go far. Barry was curled up in his study, his head mashed to a pulp. He'd been bludgeoned to death. A golf iron lay nearby, dripping with blood and brain matter. I must've just missed the killer."

"You went home to wash the handkerchief before going to Barry Burns' place?"

"Yes," Malcolm said, hanging his head. "If I'd gone straight there I might have been in time to prevent his death."

"Or you might have become victim number five."

"True. That's what might have happened to Valerie. You know, wrong place, wrong time sort of thing. Well, I went into the bathroom, wet a tissue, and wiped off the letters on Barry's forehead, but these weren't so legible because there wasn't much left of his face. I flushed the tissue down the loo and called the police from the phone on his desk."

Rex grunted his disapproval. "And then?" he asked with increasing dread.

"I went outside to wait for the police. That's when I noticed that Vic Chandler's door was open across the street. I sort of had a hunch, so I went over and entered his house. I felt as though I were living some awful nightmare. You have no idea … This time I had to go all the way upstairs. I didn't get a whiff of chloroform this time—"

"Chloroform?" Rex asked in surprise.

"I forgot to mention … In the first two houses, Ernest's and Barry's, I was aware of the smell of chloroform in the air. Faint, but unmistakable. You know, that sweet, sickly odour."

Rex didn't really know. But then, he wasn't a doctor. "What else might you have you forgotten to mention?"

"Nothing."

"Nothing else seemed unusual at the crime scenes other than the nature of the murders?" Rex prodded.

"Not really. Everything appeared to have been left in good order—except for the bodies, I mean. No signs of ransacking or anything like that. Now that you mention it, though, I did notice a brochure tucked into Ernest's waistband. I thought it an odd place to put it, but old people do odd things, don't they? I only noticed it because he was lying on the floor and his cardigan had fallen open."

"What was on the brochure?" Rex asked.

"From what I could see, it was advertising a timeshare in Marbella."

"Spain. Very nice. Anything else oot of place in the room or in the garage, or at Barry's house before we go on?"

"Nothing that sticks out," Malcolm replied, shaking his head with conviction.

"So, after you arrived at Vic Chandler's house, you went upstairs…"

"I did, and there was Vic Chandler in the bath."

"Dead, I take it."

"Indeed. In his birthday suit, the tub full of water."

"Drowned?"

Malcolm shook his head again. "According to Dr. Hewitt, the pathologist who performed the autopsy and an erstwhile colleague of mine, drowning was not the cause of death. There was no water in the victim's lungs and no asphyxia from a dry drowning. He was electrocuted."

"What with?"

"An electric razor was found in the bath. These are older homes; well, over a quarter of a century old. Some of the wall sockets are not earthed. Two hundred and forty volts of electricity combined with water is a lethal combination. I've seen several deaths in my day caused by people dropping a radio in the bath or else standing up in one and switching on a light."

"I don't suppose Vic Chandler could have electrocuted himself accidentally while shaving in the bath?"

Malcolm shook his head with regret. "The letters…"

"Written in blood on his forehead?"

His friend nodded. "But his head was partially submerged and they were all but washed away. So I left well alone."

"Thank heaven for small mercies," Rex said dryly.

Malcolm responded with a wan smile. "Yes, that was a relief."

"But the police will never know what was written there if they don't know what to look for." Rex paused while he thought about the scene in the bathroom. "Is there enough current in an electric razor to electrocute someone?" he asked.

"Apparently."

"Did you mention the chloroform to the police?"

"Of course I did."

Of course, Rex said to himself. "Safe, maybe, to assume the killer overcame his victims with chloroform before he guillotined, battered, and asphyxiated them to death in the first three instances," he told Malcolm. "But he or she had to gain entry first. The two older victims likely looked though their peepholes. Elderly people tend to be more careful aboot that sort of thing. I read in one of the papers that their exterior doors had deadbolts on them and they'd taken extra precautions to secure the windows."

"Sounds like they were a bit paranoid," Malcolm remarked.

"And rightly so, as it transpires. Now, Vic Chandler was already in his bath, so he was a captive audience, so to speak. The killer may have got in through an unlocked door or window, or else picked a lock, and left afterwards through the front door. Perhaps Vic wasn't as careful as the older men." Rex took a sip of coffee from his mug, a souvenir from Tenerife festooned with palm trees, and as incongruous to the cold, wet weather outside as were the exotic destinations of Helen's ocean cruise. He hoped his fiancée was enjoying her time off from her sometimes-stressful job as a school counsellor. He shook himself free of these distractions and reverted his attention to Malcolm and the mess he had put himself in.

"As for Valerie Trotter...," Rex mused aloud, "was she already at Ernest's house or did she arrive after his murder? Did the killer answer the door to her? That's a chilling thought. And was it just the one killer, I wonder? One killer, two victims would be a feat, even if one of them was an octogenarian. And what is the significance of those letters?" So many questions.

Malcolm looked uncomfortable again at the mention of this evidence, as well he might, Rex thought, before saying, "In view of the fact all four victims had the same letters written on their foreheads, we can safely conclude this was murder in each case and not suicide. Not to mention the nature of the deaths. After all, beating oneself to a pulp is not the easiest way to go."

"And if you write on your forehead, won't the letters appear back to front and the wrong way round?" Malcolm asked. He mimicked writing the letters *M*, *N*, and *P* on his forehead. "The *P* could even be the number nine."

"I've never written on my forehead." Rex tried the same experiment. "Depends which side you start from, I suppose."

"Then there's the mirror effect," Malcolm said. "Like on the front of ambulances which say, *ECNALUBMA*, so that when you read the word in your rear view mirror it appears normal."

"In this case, the letters appeared normal to the naked eye?"

"Exactly as though someone else had written on the bodies. Except for the *N*, which was the wrong way round, or flipped, if you will."

"*N*, as in your middle initial. Remind me what it stands for again. Nigel or Norman?"

"Norman."

"Strange that one letter should appear different." Rex gave a perplexed sigh. "Wish you could have at least taken a photo. Are you sure you remember correctly?"

"Perfectly sure."

"Good. Report all this to the police. Tonight."

"Just give it two days. Then I'll go to DCI Cooper myself. I won't even involve you."

"Two days can make a huge difference in a case. The police need this information. I don't suppose you know through the grapevine if the house agent has actually confessed to the murders?"

"Not that I know of." Malcolm threw up his hands. "What else could M-N-P stand for, if not my name?" he asked in a pleading voice. "Can't we at least find an alternative to present to the police first? What if Chris Walker wanted to implicate me?"

"Why would he?"

"I don't know. I never had any dealings with him."

"But you met him?"

"Briefly. Mostly I just saw him around the community going about his house-selling business."

"M-N-P. could be an acronym for something. And you're sure aboot the letters?" Rex demanded again.

"Unfortunately, yes."

"One thing occurs to me." Rex leaned back in his recliner, cupping his mug of coffee in both hands. "If this house agent has no criminal past, I don't see how he could have executed four very different methods of murder so flawlessly. I'd say our killer was a pro."

Malcolm nodded agreement. "But Walker could have a violent past. At first I thought it couldn't be him, but who else would know my initials? These agents look through databases and phone books for prospects."

"You need to stop being so paranoid."

"Well, you have to admit, it's a horrible coincidence, Rex."

"It is, but we can't let it cloud our thinking."

"Can you find out from the police what they know?"

"You'd be in a better position to do that. You've liaised with them in your professional life."

"I'd rather keep a low profile in view of, well, you know."

"Your perversion of justice? Aye, well, we need to rectify that pronto." Rex tipped the dregs of his coffee down his throat and reached for his jacket.

"Wait. Please," Malcolm pleaded. "There has to be a way out."

"There isn't."

"But if we can find out whether Chris Walker is the right man or if someone else is responsible, we might not have to bring up the letters at all."

"The police have far greater resources than we do to look into forensic stuff," Rex objected. He paused in thought. "However, I do have a contact who might prove useful in procuring information, if necessary."

"Oh, aye?" Malcolm asked hopefully. "A legal acquaintance?"

"A law clerk by the name of Thaddeus, who hasn't failed me yet. But that doesn't solve the problem of your interfering with the crime scenes."

"I know. I feel a huge responsibility in this case. That's why I called you. I want to make sure the police convict the right person. In any case," Malcolm added in desperation, "going to the police with our information doesn't in any way guarantee Walker's release, if he's in jail."

Our information, Rex repeated to himself, mentally fuming. Malcolm was all but including him in his deplorable actions. "What exactly do the police have on Chris Walker?" he asked. He left his jacket on his lap, pausing for an answer before putting it on to accompany Malcolm to the police station.

"They haven't even released his name to the media. All I know is culled from local gossip. Mrs. Parsons in Otter Court knows the receptionist at the firm Walker owns, and she told Lottie the fact the victims all had their properties listed with him—including Valerie Trotter, although she alone wasn't murdered in her home—made the detectives suspicious. That and the fact they would have invited him into their home without a second thought."

"There must be more to it than that," Rex said. "House agents aren't in the habit of murdering their clients. They rely on them for their commissions. Perhaps the detectives found something troubling in his background check: Time in prison or a psychiatric institution. I wonder if any other seller will be targeted while he's under police scrutiny. That would be his best defence."

Malcolm gave a sigh of relief. "That's why I needed you here. To map it all out objectively."

The word "map" reminded Rex of something. "Why is it Notting Hamlet is so hard to find?"

"I don't know. Some pranksters keep moving the signs about or removing them altogether. We have an undesirable element around here. Loud bikers and dogs."

Rex was amused to hear bikers and dogs put in the same category, but Malcolm appeared deadly serious. "Is that why so many homes are up for sale, assuming the spate of For Sale signs predates the murders?" he asked his friend.

"Seven. Ten per cent of the total number of homes. But you know what people are like. Sheep. They suddenly get scared they'll miss out and get left behind. But a high volume of signs devalues the properties. The homeowners are all trying to undercut each other."

"Chris Walker must have been in clover—before he ended up in hot water."

"Oh, he was exploiting the situation, telling everyone it was time to move out and get into a newer property. The sellers, quite frankly, can't tolerate the increase in noise pollution."

"That bad?"

"Dogs barking like you wouldn't believe. Motorcycles with modified pipes that sound like Boeing jets. And it used to be such a peaceful community," Malcolm said wistfully. "A lot of homemakers and retirees with time to spend on their gardens and organize neighbourly events like barbeques and fêtes on the green … Jocelyn was very involved."

"She was a remarkable gifted woman," Rex reminisced along with him.

"It's not the same without her. Not just for me. All of Notting Hamlet suffered when she passed away."

"I remember her funeral was very well-attended."

Malcolm indicated Rex's jacket lying in transit across his lap. "Can we at least wait until morning?" he asked, looking lost and dejected.

Rex took pity on his bereaved friend. "Fair enough," he relented. "It's getting late and I'm ready for bed."

"I'll show you around the Hamlet tomorrow, give you a better picture."

"That would be helpful. Shame you don't have a dog we could walk. It would be a good way to meet people and get information."

Malcolm reacted cheerfully to the suggestion. "Mr. Olson, who's currently bedridden, has a nice black Lab that needs walking. The neighbours take it in turns to help out."

"I like Labs. And I need the exercise. What's the dog's name?"

"Magic."

"Well, let's see what magic he can conjure up for us," Rex said. They would certainly need it. It appeared someone didn't want any sellers leaving Notting Hamlet and preferred to see them dead.

FIVE

MAGIC PROVED TO BE getting on in years, much like his owner, but like most Labradors was eager to please and obediently followed Rex on his lead, his black tail wagging obligingly. Malcolm had gone to "turn himself in" as he put it, and almost two hours later had not returned. Before leaving, he had given Rex a tour of Notting Hamlet in his car, pointing out where the murders had taken place. Police tape still girded the homes of Ernest Blackwell, Barry Burns, and Vic Chandler, a reminder that crime had made multiple visits to Notting Hamlet.

The community was essentially T-shaped, with a cul-de-sac at each end of the top bar. A square, referred to as "the green," stood in between the cul-de-sacs, bucolically named Badger Court and Otter Court respectively. These backed onto the River Ivel, a tributary of the Great Ouse, and contained the most prestigious properties, due to the water views, though even with all the rain this part of the river was narrow, as Rex had noted from his bedroom window. Barry Burns and Vic Chandler had met their deaths in Badger

Court, Malcolm's cul-de-sac west of the square. Mostly surrounded by evergreens, it afforded privacy and shelter from the wind, not to mention ample cover for an intruder bent on murder.

The developer had continued his wildlife theme by designating the street leading from the square to the entrance as Fox Lane. This, the sole vehicle access to the community, was approached from the south side by Notting Hamlet Road, which ran through open countryside, the fields and gently undulating hills interspersed with copses of bare trees. As far as developments went, Notting Hamlet had been well-planned, and its drawback of residing off the beaten track had no doubt been exploited as a selling point to those seeking peace and tranquillity in a rural setting. This much Rex had been able to ascertain from his car tour with Malcolm.

His friend lived four houses into Badger Court on the river side. As Rex stood with the dog on the overgrown bank contemplating the Ivel winding away to a thread, the wind buffeted him in sporadic gusts. The frigid blasts ruffled the glassy surface of the water into sharp waves that, after each onslaught, resolved into a slow current downstream, carrying along twigs and litter and sodden leaves. A cold, fusty odour came off the river, adding to the inhospitable atmosphere. The air, laden with humidity, promised more rain. Drowned in uniform grey, the horizon beyond the barren fields and misty meadows blurred into an ashen sky as fog enveloped the landscape.

Continuing his reconnoitring expedition along the banks, Rex saw nothing of interest, except for a few squirrels, which the black Labrador didn't even attempt to pursue. Malcolm was one of Magic's regular walkers, and Rex, who had always wanted a dog, had been glad to take over, especially as he harboured ulterior motives.

However, due to the inclement weather, he had yet to meet anyone else out with their dog, though he heard strident barking erupt from a house on Fox Lane as he passed by with the Lab. Magic did not respond to the provocation. The home of the vociferous canines stood three doors down from Ernest Blackwell's, towards the northern end of the row of detached homes.

The rain of the night before had left a sheen on the roofs and roads. The front lawns remained sodden, while puddles glistened at the foot of the driveways. The chill damp permeated Rex's exposed skin, and he adjusted the soft wool scarf around his neck, which was still stiff from his drive from Scotland the day before.

Where the devil had Malcolm got to, he wondered, glancing at his watch. Had he been arrested for withholding evidence? Rex had insisted on accompanying him to the police station in an unofficial capacity, but Malcolm had convinced him he would be fine and would call on his mobile phone if the detective in charge of the case proved "unsympathetic." Unsympathetic, Rex echoed, with a shake of his head. Clearly, Malcolm did not comprehend the enormity of his actions.

Magic's tail was beginning to flag and the dog was looking at him in a questioning way, as if to ask if they were going to walk much further.

"Right, old boy, home!" Rex announced, taking pity on the poor animal.

Magic cocked his ears at the word "home" and gave a short, high-pitched bark. Rex felt less enthusiastic. While the walk had provided him with much needed exercise and a useful perspective regarding the layout of Notting Hamlet and its points of access and egress, he had failed to run into any of the residents as he had hoped. Then, just as he was crossing the street in the direction of Mr. Olson's house, he spotted an elderly woman in a heavy tweed coat and blue bonnet, carrying a string bag of groceries.

"Morning," Rex called out. "Not the best weather to be oot and aboot, is it?"

"Ghastly," she replied. "You must be Malcolm's friend from Scotland. He mentioned you'd be staying for a few days."

Rex did not know what else Malcolm had told her and so did not volunteer any information beyond his name in the form of an introduction.

"Lottie Green," the woman reciprocated, shaking his outstretched hand with her mitted one. She stooped to pat the dog. "He's a love," she said. "Nice you're doing a neighbour a good turn. I'm taking some shopping to Mrs. Marbles. She's bedridden too, from a stroke."

While she prattled on, Rex thanked his lucky stars that he had chanced to meet the person who'd spied Ernest Blackwell through the window. He was wondering how best to elicit information without revealing his vested interest in the case when she spared him the trouble by asking, "I suppose you heard about our murders?"

"Indeed."

"Thank goodness they caught the killer, or I wouldn't be out on the street by myself. Of course, my house is not up for sale. That was the connection, you see."

Magic sat down patiently on the damp pavement, tongue lolling and drooling.

"Aye, most curious. And Malcolm said you were the first person to find the body, or, at least, alert anybody."

"I was," Lottie said with relish, her wizened rosy cheeks putting Rex in mind of an old apple. "I've been interviewed many times by the police and the media, even got on the telly! Of course, I had no idea it was a murder at the time. Ernest had a weak ticker, so at first I thought it was a heart attack. And he was a martyr to his arthritis, too. If I hadn't seen his feet sticking out from under the piano, who knows how long it would have been until someone found him? And Valerie Trotter. Or the other two. Malcolm went to tell Barry about his friend's death, and found him dead as well! And Vic Chandler, and all!" Bundled up against the cold, the elderly woman appeared impervious to the damp chill, and yet Rex, in good conscience, could not keep her chatting on the street any longer.

"Here, let me help you with your bag," he offered, holding out his arm.

"Oh, no need. It's not heavy. Just a few tins of soup, a loaf of bread, and some greens. And where is Malcolm? I saw him leave in his car early this morning."

"He, ehm, went to the police station."

"He's a key witness, of course, and, being a doctor and all, the police must have a lot of questions. I suppose they're busy making a case against the house agent and have to get all their facts straight. No one understands why he did it. Two old men and a woman who never hurt a soul in their lives. Vic Chandler served in Belfast, so he probably did, but only in the line of duty."

"Aye. Most mysterious. Did you know them well?" Rex asked, careful to dissimulate the extent of his curiosity, though Lottie seemed happy to gossip. He began to entertain the suspicion that she had peeked through a pair of net curtains and sought him out on the street. At this point, Magic yawned and hunkered down on his forepaws, as though resigned to an extended conversation between the humans.

"Well, they've all lived here as long as I have, going on twenty years," Lottie said. "Ernest was very sociable, but I got the impression he was not someone you'd want to cross. Barry now, he was a nice man, a bit of a dandy. Essex boys, both of them, with a gift of the gab, though Barry wore a hearing aid and didn't always hear right."

"And the other two?"

"Vic was younger, somewhere in his late fifties. Kept himself fit. He'd been in the army, done a few tours in Northern Ireland. Had a nasty scar down his face and a missing pinkie. Now, Valerie was a bit loud, if you know what I mean. Loud voice, loud makeup, but her heart was in the right place."

"Did they all know each other?" Rex asked casually.

"Not more than anyone else, that I know of. As I told the reporters, we're a friendly community, for the most part. *Were.* The residents near the entrance on Owl Lane are riff-raff and we don't like to include them, but it's hard to ignore that street." Lottie wrinkled her tiny nose. "But that problem is nothing compared to the murders. Oh dear, those have really put Notting Hamlet on the map!"

"I wonder how many more For Sale signs will go up," Rex said. "I've counted six or seven on my walk and, curiously, one was turned around, facing towards the house. And I've seen a home with the windows shuttered up, so I thought it was vacant, but a man came out and scowled at me when I walked by!"

"The man at forty-five?" Lottie asked, pointing up the street. "He's a strange one. Doesn't say much except to complain about the dogs next door. Says their barking drills through the walls. I admit, the one dog makes you want to grit your teeth, its bark is so ear-piercing. It's not even a big dog. Couldn't tell you what breed it is.

Mr. Woods is in a right hurry to move, especially now, I shouldn't wonder."

"I'd be too. Terrible business. But it looks like the police got their man," Rex trolled.

Lottie took the bait. "Can't un-ring the bell though, can you? I mean, four murders. Notting Hamlet will never be the same again. The victims had to have known who they were opening the door to. They'd not have thought twice about letting their house agent in."

Rex nodded, but he knew there had to be more evidence than that to book Chris Walker. As far as he knew, the house agent hadn't been arrested yet. "You didn't happen to see anything unusual the day of the murders? I mean, before you saw Ernest under the piano?"

"Not really. I do remember it was very wet that day. I was getting ready to have my elevenses and had the kettle on, and I was thinking I might close the curtains in the sitting room, it was so gloomy out. I remember thinking nobody would be out in that weather unless they had urgent business. Well, an hour later, I realized my ginger tom was still outside. I expected to find him waiting on the doorstep. When he wasn't there, I went looking for him. I saw a BMW pass by and thought the rain would spoil its shiny exterior."

"What colour?"

"Blue or green is what I told the police. Teal, I suppose it might have been."

"Does Chris Walker own a BMW?"

"No, he has a white car, but I couldn't tell you what make. I'm not very good with cars."

"What direction was the BMW going?"

"Up Fox Lane." Lottie looked heavenward. "Looks like the rain might start again at any moment. I best get on. I can't think of anything else that might help you, but I'll call if I remember anything. Malcolm said you're a Crown prosecutor in Edinburgh and like to follow murder cases."

"Morbid, isn't it?" Rex apologized. "But the truth of the matter is I hadn't seen Malcolm in a while and I was overdue for a visit. He's been talking aboot the murders and, well, now I'm hooked!"

"Oh, I know! I'm glued to the telly. Of course, the news will move on to other topics eventually. You should have been here that first week. News vans and reporters everywhere! They'll pick up again for the trial."

Lottie seemed convinced of Walker's guilt and inevitable conviction, and Rex decided not to disabuse her at this time, in the absence of other suspects. "Well, don't let me detain you any longer. Are you sure you don't want help with your shopping?"

"Oh no. As I said, it's quite light and I'm stronger than I look!"

The dog whined at that moment. "Right, well, I should get this one home," Rex said. "Come on, boy!"

Magic struggled to his feet and wagged his tail. Rex led him back to Mr. Olson's house, where the old man's Jamaican caregiver took possession of the dog and thanked the Scotsman in his clipped, sing-song voice.

Rex walked back up Fox Lane, past Ernest Blackwell's house, which bore a muted, inverted aspect, as though in mourning for its owner. A few doors up, the house once belonging to Valerie Trotter presented a similar impression.

As he crossed the street leading east and west to the cul-de-sacs, he spotted a lean youth hunched in a hooded jacket, hands jammed in the pockets, leaving Otter Court. His eyes, wary and darkly circled in a pale face, avoided Rex's. The lone figure turned onto the green and skulked along the brick path to the river. Rex made a mental note to ask Malcolm about this curious individual.

He checked his phone even though he would have heard it ring. The screen remained blank. Perhaps no call from Malcolm meant good news. His friend would only have made contact if he required his assistance in extricating himself from the situation he had so stupidly placed himself in. Rex felt a fresh wave of irritation against Malcolm for complicating the case, and yet he felt all the more determined to get to the bottom of the neighbourhood murders.

SIX

Rex saw Malcolm's car parked in his open garage and hastened his step, anxious to find out how his friend had fared at the station. He had covered half the driveway when a male voice hailed him from the other side of the hedge where, upon turning around, Rex spotted a man of about sixty in a flat cap pruning the foliage.

"Staying long in our parts?" the man enquired in a jovial tone. "You're a brave one."

Rex smiled and said he thought he was quite old and big enough to take care of himself.

"I'm sure Vic Chandler thought the same. He was a bouncer at a nightclub in Godminton, but his muscle and army training didn't do the poor sod any good in the end." Malcolm's neighbour looked toward the remnant of blue and white police tape fluttering in the doorway of the victim's house on the other side of the cul-de-sac. "Win Prendergast." He stuck out his hand across the soggy hedge.

Rex had heard about Winston Prendergast from Malcolm: A busybody bachelor constantly giving advice on how best to wash a car or mow a lawn. The neighbour on Malcolm's other side had gone into a retirement home. Her daughter was going to move in the house with her family once they had finished uprooting their life in Shropshire. For now it stood empty, and Malcolm had been cutting her grass to maintain a tidy appearance.

Rex introduced himself in turn. "Pleased to make your acquaintance," he told Prendergast.

"Visiting from Edinburgh, I hear. I'm a Clanger myself, Bedfordshire born and bred," the man said proudly. "Known Malcolm long?"

"Since university."

"I suppose he filled you in on the murders? We've all been on edge, wondering which of our neighbours could have slaughtered our four residents. There are crimes that still merit the death penalty, if you ask me." Clearly, Prendergast was the sort of person who gave an opinion whether it was requested or not. "Why should tax payers fork out their hard-earned income to house and feed such scum? A dog shouldn't have to suffer what happened to those four."

"Did you know them well?" Rex asked with sympathetic interest.

"Well enough. Played golf with Ernest and Barry. And with Vic Chandler once or twice, but he didn't have the patience for it. Ernest had focus and a good swing for his age. Barry was hit-and-miss. I think his deafness threw him a bit off balance."

"But it's not all aboot the game, is it?" Rex said, not an avid golfer himself, but having played back home in Edinburgh and in St. Andrews on occasion. "A beer or two at the club with your mates after a round is a pleasant way to spend the day."

"I won't argue with that. And Ernest was a character. He could tell a funny story and have you in stitches, right enough. Came from running a pub, I suppose. Barry was sociable too, a proper gentle-man, but, like I said, he was hearing-impaired, so sometimes it was hard to keep a conversation going with him. And Ernest had memory lapses. Senile dementia, I believe they call it. They were getting on a bit, of course. But for all that, they weren't at death's door, until someone pushed them through it."

"What was Barry's background?" Rex asked with a more-than-friendly curiosity.

Prendergast jutted out his thick lips while he reflected. "I think he said he had an auto-repair shop. Vic was in insurance."

"And the female victim? Did you know her at all?"

"Saw her about, but never to talk to."

Rex could think of nothing else to ask without appearing ghoul-ish, so he bid Prendergast good day and strode up the rest of the driveway. He called out his friend's name upon opening the front door with his spare key and unbuttoned his coat.

"I'm in the kitchen," Malcolm replied.

Rex deposited his overcoat and brolly on the coat tree and headed in that direction. "Well?" he asked Malcolm, who was busying him-self with the kettle.

"Well, I'm still a free man."

"I can see that. What happened?"

"I spoke to DCI Cooper, who's heading up the investigation, and explained that I had remembered something about the first body. I told him about what had looked like three letters scrawled across Ernest Blackwell's forehead—the M, back-to-front N, and P—but that I accidentally erased them when administering to the patient."

"Dead patient. You said Mr. Blackwell was all but decapitated."

"One must always check for a pulse. It's a reflex."

"Like wiping away evidence?"

Malcolm had the grace to look ashamed. "Look, I did what I said I would," he replied defensively. "The detective said he would ask Walker about the letters, but didn't seem to take it too seriously."

Or perhaps he did not take Malcolm too seriously, Rex reflected. Detective Chief Inspector Cooper may have concluded that Malcolm was trying to stay involved in the case out of a sense of self-importance or curiosity. "And you didn't press it?" he enquired of his friend.

"No, why would I? It's his job to decide whether it's important or not. I did ask whether Chris Walker was dyslexic."

"And what did he say?"

"He said he would review Walker's statement, but that he didn't recall the house agent's writing to be better or worse than most. Perhaps some capitals inserted for small letters, but it had been legible, he said, even if the prose would never be nominated for a Pulitzer."

"Very amusing," Rex retorted. "And did you happen to mention your initials on the other victims' foreheads?"

"He didn't ask." Malcolm fidgeted with the tea towel he had used on the counter to mop up spilt water from the kettle.

"Malcolm!"

"Listen, Rex. He's certain they've got the right man. At Ernest Blackwell's house they found a damp shoe print on the front doormat matching Walker's, which puts him at the scene at around the time the murder was committed. It started raining late in the morning that day and my medical colleague estimated time of death at approximately noon."

"Were Walker's shoe prints found in the back room by the piano?"

"No," Malcolm replied cautiously. "Just on the mat, apparently. He may have removed his shoes out of courtesy before walking down the hall. A good house agent would think to do that."

"Aye, or else he didn't go further than the front door mat, and someone else was padding around in their socks. Did they find blood on Walker's clothes? With all that blood, it's unlikely he'd get away squeaky clean."

"Don't know if they did or not. The only other shoe prints belonged to me," Malcolm said with an air of apology. "It was still raining when I got there." He put the filled teapot and two mugs on the kitchen table, along with a tin of digestive biscuits.

The two men sat down across from each other, and Rex asked what Malcolm had been doing when Lottie phoned to tell him about Ernest lying on the carpet.

"I stayed indoors that Thursday as it was pouring outside. Caught up on some medical journals."

Malcolm's answer seemed a bit pat to Rex, but he let it go for now while his friend served the tea. Rex deplored the fact Malcolm had not come completely clean about the letters written in blood. He brought that point up again with as much tact as his patience would allow.

"If the inspector had pressed for more information," Malcolm told him, "I would have mentioned the possibility of letters on the other victims."

"Possibility?" With an indignant sigh, Rex heaped three teaspoons of sugar into his mug.

"Vic Chandler was in the bath, remember. The steam had blurred the letters. And Barry Burns's face was so beaten in, the blood could have said anything."

"Lottie said Barry was something of a dandy," Rex said, deviating from Malcolm's excuses for his behaviour, since he couldn't take much more of them for now.

"I suppose he was," his friend said, gazing into space. "Tall and trim, with a full head of white hair, which he kept longish, probably the way he had it in his younger days. A bit frail, though, and hard of hearing."

"So Lottie and your neighbour said. Prendergast waylaid me as I was walking up the driveway," Rex explained.

Malcolm nodded and grinned. "What a gasbag. I bet he gave you the lowdown on all the neighbours."

"Mainly the victims. And what aboot Vic Chandler? All Win could tell me was that he had no patience for golf and had been in the insurance business. What was he like?"

"Didn't know him that well, just saw him from time to time across the street. He liked to potter in his shed round the back of his house. Kept himself to himself mostly. Not very tall, but barrel-chested, with powerful shoulders. And he shaved his head, I think because he was going bald on top."

"Injured in Belfast, I hear."

"He had a scar on one side of his face that dragged his eye down a bit and gave him a sinister look, and he had a missing finger on his right hand."

"A tough-looking character. I remember the picture in the paper. And the woman, Valerie ... On the blousy side, you said?"

Malcolm nodded. "Attractive in a barmaid sort of way. I could see her and Ernest having an affair, at a pinch. Though quite a bit older, he had charisma."

He seemed relieved to have the focus off himself, but Rex was not prepared to let his evidence tampering go that easily. "What if the letters have greater significance than you let on to the inspector? Did he notice the connection between them and your initials?"

Malcolm swallowed down a bite of biscuit. "Not immediately. After all, that middle letter was not a proper N. Later in the interview, though, he asked why Walker might have wanted to frame me."

Very astute of the detective, Rex thought. "And you said?"

"I barely knew the chap. I had one conversation with him when he was putting the For Sale sign in Barry's garden. I asked if the homes in the neighbourhood had gone up in value in the past year, and he said it depended on how quickly you wanted to sell. Apparently, Barry was in a hurry."

"Do you know why?"

"You'd have to ask Walker."

"That might be difficult, considering his situation," Rex said pointedly.

Malcolm expelled a long breath. "Look, he confessed to being there that Thursday."

"And killing Ernest Blackwell?"

"No, why would he? If he has a good barrister, he could still go free."

No thanks to you, Rex said to himself. "So, if you're so convinced now he's guilty, why do you need me?"

Malcolm shifted in his chair. "I thought you could shed some light on the murders one way or the other, and, to tell the truth"—he glanced quickly at Rex—"my conscience was bothering me. I feel rather better now that I've made a clean breast of it at the station but, I'll admit, I was terrified. Do you think the detective will call me back in?"

Rex thought it more than probable. No detective, particularly of Cooper's rank, would risk his reputation and the case by not following up on a lead, however late in the proceedings. And this case was only three weeks old. Where did this leave him in his own investigation, he wondered. What did he actually have to go on, and was his time and effort wasted if Chris Walker was the culprit?

"We could try to determine why the house agent might have wanted to frame me," Malcolm said.

"It would help if there were other suspects. Are there no other people of interest the police could be looking at?"

"There was a handyman, but he was eliminated when his alibi checked out. He does odd jobs for Mrs. Parsons and told her he was originally the prime suspect, on account of his having done work for all the victims when they were getting their homes ready for sale. You know, all the deferred maintenance stuff. Chris Walker had told the owners to address the problems up front, so the homes would show better and there'd be no delays later on. So Randall, whom we refer to as Handy Randy, was over at their homes doing some paint and electrical jobs. Ernest and Barry were too old to get up a ladder. And Vic had a fear of heights."

"A solid alibi?" Rex asked regretfully. A handyman would know the victims' floor plans and their routines, and would have ready access to the homes. He might even have had an opportunity to copy the door keys or else knew where spares were kept.

"Pretty solid. The day of the murders he was visiting his mother in Bedford, twenty-five minutes away, depending on traffic. The security cameras at the old people's home recorded his coming and going. That's what let him off the hook."

Rex sat back in his chair, deep in thought for a moment. "A whole day is a long time to spend with a senile person. Unlikely they'd be alert the whole time. He could have slipped out a side door for a few hours. An hour to return to Notting Hamlet and back again, and an hour or so more to commit the murders. Aye," he concluded, "it would take a bit of doing and a good deal of luck not to be spotted. But it's feasible. What's this handyman like?"

"Let's see … mid-forties, a bit rough around the edges, with a swarthy complexion and blue eyes that some women swoon over. Rumour has it he and Valerie had something going on. Him being married with three kids made for juicy gossip."

"Does he drive a bluish-green BMW?"

Malcolm barked out a laugh. "Hardly. He has an old van."

"Where does he live?"

"On that row of homes down by the entrance."

"Oh, so here in Notting Hamlet," Rex said with interest.

Malcolm sighed in frustration. "I wish Owl Lane didn't exist at all. It's an eyesore. You don't notice so much coming in, but when you leave, you can't help but see all the junk. The homes are not kept up to the same level as the rest in the community. Some are let out and, well, tenants just don't take the same pride in where they live, do they? Some of us have tried to get the owners to do something about the detracting aspect of Owl Lane, but most of it falls on deaf ears. The bikers chase off the petitioners. Big Bill's the worst offender. He runs a motorcycle repair shop out of his garage in flagrant contravention of zoning regulations."

Malcolm would no doubt have continued to vent had Rex not stopped him. Discussing petty feuds within the community might not be the most effective use of their time, he argued. And yet, the murder of four residents did speak to some form of vendetta. "If we could determine why the victims were killed, it would no doubt help us discover who did it," he told Malcolm. "We need to learn more about the victims. Who else was or might still be on the police suspect list?" he asked. "Specifically people with a grudge."

"Don't know about a grudge," Malcolm replied. "As far as I'm aware, Randy didn't have issues with Ernest or the others about not getting paid, for instance. And I never heard any complaints about his work or stuff going missing, and he did a lot of repairs around the community. Anyway, nothing was reported stolen from the victims' homes. The police questioned the postman, utility workers, all the delivery people coming into the community, people who had left suddenly after the event…"

"Were there any?"

"There were some who went to stay with friends or relatives until the perpetrator was caught. But no really suspicious absences that I know of."

"Sounds like the police have been quite thorough."

"They're still questioning people in the community. Shall I make more tea?" Malcolm asked, lifting the earthenware pot. "This is almost empty and it must be stone cold by now."

"Aye, why not?"

While Malcolm prepared a fresh pot, Rex ruminated over the lack of suspects other than Chris Walker. And yet, where was the smoking gun? No bloody shoeprints had been found, only a damp one on the front door mat. The house agent might have come by to update Ernest on some potential interest or to discuss a price reduction, or any number of items related to the property.

Rex wished he could eliminate the bloody letters from the equation. However, they must hold some degree of significance if the killer had smeared them on the victims. Vicious murder had clearly been the intent and not burglary. If only Malcolm had not acted out of paranoia and washed the letters away. Rex could not help but feel disappointed in his friend and frustrated that neither he nor the police had a full set of facts.

Malcolm sat down and placed the teapot on the quilted mat. Rex watched, distracted. The ringing of the phone in the hall interrupted his sequence of thoughts. Malcolm jumped up to answer it, panic written all over his face.

"Do you think it's DCI Cooper?" he asked.

"There's only one way to find oot."

"Right." His friend visibly braced himself and marched into the hall.

SEVEN

Rex heard a hesitant "Hello?" from Malcolm and then his relieved voice saying, "Oh, Lottie, dear ... Yes, he is. One moment. It's for you," he called out to Rex. "Lottie," he said covering the mouthpiece with his hand as Rex approached. "She says she remembered something."

"Good. Let's hope it's something worthwhile," Rex said under his breath. He took the phone. "Lottie, you have something for me?"

"Well, it might be something or nothing. I was going over our conversation while I was Hoovering the living room and for some reason I remembered some weeks back Ernest saying it was time for him and Frankie to move on. He seemed troubled. This was when I was asking about the For Sale sign in his garden. Soon after that, Barry Burns, Vic Chandler, and Valerie Trotter all put their homes on the market. The first sign to go up was that horrible man's at Forty-Five Fox Lane. We were all relieved when that happened. Then the woman up the road, Charlotte what's-her-name, put her house up for sale. After the murders, it was the Ballantines' home, under a different house agent. I'm sure more will follow."

Rex was wondering where all this was going when Lottie said, "Anyway, I didn't know who Frankie was. I thought maybe it was his cat or a hamster. I'd never set foot in his house, so I didn't know if he had a pet. It could have been a goldfish for all I know. He didn't have any children. I was about to ask him, but his phone rang and he hurried inside to get it. To my knowledge, no pet was found when the police came to investigate his murder."

"Frankie could be a woman's name, couldn't it?" Rex asked. "Short for Francesca."

"Shame to change such a pretty name," Lottie remarked.

"I changed mine from Reginald."

"In your case, Rex is better."

"Thank you. And thanks for that bit of information. I'll ask Malcolm if he knows of anyone by the name of Frankie." He turned to Malcolm, who shook his head in the negative. "Did you talk to Ernest again after that?" Rex enquired of Lottie.

"About a week later. I recall him telling me he might have buyers for the house. He said he'd had several people look at it, but no real interest until a young couple came along."

"A young couple?"

"Yes. That's all he told me. But he seemed pleased. He was eager to move. Something about wanting to be closer to his sister in Cheshire. I'm afraid that's all I can tell you. But this couple might be able to give you some information about Chris Walker."

"Did the police interview them?" Rex asked.

"I don't know. I didn't think to mention it to the police. They were mainly interested in what I witnessed through the window and what happened after that. Does it help you?"

"I'm not sure yet, Lottie, but it's more than I had before. Thanks again for indulging me in my little hobby."

"Oh, not at all! I'll see if I can come up with any more titbits."

"You might want to contact DCI Cooper about what you told me."

"Oh, I don't like *him*! Very superior, that one. Do you suppose the couple have bad things to say about Chris Walker? Oh, I'm sure the police have already questioned everyone connected with him."

Rex never felt it safe to assume. With very little of his own to go on, he now had a line of inquiry, however tenuous. He warmly bid Lottie goodbye and replaced the handset on the old rotary phone.

"What was all that about?" Malcolm asked, leaning up against the wall with his arms crossed.

"A young couple were interested in Ernest Blackwell's house. Lottie thought they might have something on Walker. She doesn't know if the police are aware of them."

"You think the couple might have seen something?" Malcolm asked. "You'd think they would have come forward if they had."

"Perhaps they did. Grab your coat. We're going for a walk."

"Where to?"

"The other homes up for sale, to see if the owners showed their home to a young couple."

Malcolm made no effort to move. "But …"

"It's an angle worth exploring in the absence of anything else. Better take our umbrellas in case it decides to rain again."

Armed against the weather, the two men turned onto the shining-wet street, which was deserted, except for a man opposite Malcolm's house vigorously sweeping under his covered front porch. This had been extended beyond the original plan and tiled. His bristled moustache, resembling the broom he was slamming from side to side, stood out from thirty yards away. He granted them a cordial wave and returned to his task, evidently keen to get on with it without interruption.

"He lives next door to the late Vic Chandler," Rex noted. "If he were less preoccupied, I'd go over and talk to him."

"That's Jerry Macintyre, a retired Chief Fire Officer. He was with his wife at her sister's in Bedford the day of the murders. They didn't get back until after the police had arrived. I've spoken to everybody on Badger Court. Those who weren't at work were inside because of the rain. Nobody saw anything."

"Or maybe didn't know what they saw," Rex commented, surveying the backdrop behind Vic Chandler's old property. "There are a lot of birch and oak trees back there. The killer could have used those for cover. How did Mr. Macintyre get on with his neighbour?"

"Fine, I think. Vic wasn't a man of many words. 'All right?' was his customary form of greeting. He didn't seek out anybody's company. Do you think it would be okay to take down that horrendous white dish? Jerry and I were discussing it. He says he can get his hands on a ladder tall enough to reach the roof."

"No, Malcolm! That would constitute trespassing and vandalism, and you're in enough trouble as it is. You don't know who owns that property now, and they might not appreciate you removing the satellite dish."

Malcolm looked peeved. "He should never have put it up in the first place."

Without further discussion on the matter, they crossed the cul-de-sac and made their way down Fox Lane, stopping at the shuttered mock-Tudor house whence the scowling man had emerged earlier in the day. The barricaded aspect of the property and the bleakness of the bare garden rendered number 45 less than hospitable. Malcolm told Rex he would wait at the end of the driveway, where a For Sale sign advertised the services of Walker & Associates, as did all the available properties in Notting Hamlet, bar one.

"Not a friendly man," Malcolm said by way of excuse.

"So you're letting me go into the fray on my own?"

"He may be more welcoming if you're by yourself."

"He wasn't last time. But it's too cold to be standing around arguing. What's his name again?"

"I forget. Sorry. I only know he's a chemistry teacher."

Rex referred to his notes. "Mr. Woods, according to Lottie."

He strode up the cobbled path, which felt uneven underfoot. Loosening the plaid muffler around his neck, he drilled the doorbell. Seconds later, he heard heavy footfalls approach from the inside, followed by a pause as the person presumably looked through the peephole. The door flew open.

"What d'you want?" demanded the red-faced resident, a burly man in his fifties, balding on top.

"I simply wanted to ask a few questions relating to the sale of your house, Mr. Woods. I'm not a detective or a reporter."

"Are you a buyer?"

"No, I—"

The door slammed in Rex's face, resulting in a panel of varnished wood mere inches from his nose.

"Charming," he said under his breath as he turned away and retraced his steps.

Malcolm looked gleeful. "I did warn you."

"What put a bee in his bonnet?" Rex groused.

"He's the sort of person who's irate at the entire world. He's threatened to throttle the loud dogs next door. It's been going on for a year. He's called the police and our local council, and who knows whom else. I suppose, in the end, it was just easier to move, though he must know it'll be harder to sell his property with those noisy brutes next door, not to mention the murders, and he probably feels trapped."

"The stress is obviously getting to him." Rex looked back at the hostile abode.

"You were lucky. I saw him hose down one of our resident Hells Angels who was distributing window-washing flyers. 'Get off my lawn, you effing lout!' he yelled, chasing him to his motorcycle and giving that a good dousing, too."

"I'll give him a wide berth in future."

"You should have seen the obscene gesture that long-haired hoodlum made as he drove off on his bike!" Malcolm's face grew pink with indignation. "It was Wes, Big Bill's right-hand man. He wears a studded leather dog collar and chains. Oh, how I'd love to round up the whole lot of them and send them packing."

"Inflict the bikers on someone else?" Rex retorted in good humour. "Come on. Let's try the next 'For Sale.'" They crossed the street. "This one looks more appealing, don't you think?"

Perennials planted in pebbled borders on each side of the path greeted the visitors with their cheerful splash of colour on this dreary grey day. Behind a pair of drawn curtains a lamp palely glowed, holding out hope that someone was home.

"Do you know the owners?" Rex asked Malcolm.

"I don't."

"Lottie mentioned a Charlotte."

"Lottie is a walking directory."

"She's an asset in our endeavours," Rex reminded his friend.

He pressed on the bell and stepped back beside Malcolm. The door opened, catching on a chain. A pair of green female eyes looked out, appraising them with kind interest.

"I'm Malcolm Patterson," Rex's friend said, taking the initiative. "I live on Badger Court. This is an old acquaintance of mine, Rex Graves, QC, who's conducting a private inquiry into the recent murders."

Rex presented his card through the gap in the door. The emerald eyes flicked over it.

"And what do you want with me?" asked the woman, an attractive brunette in her forties, from what Rex could see of her head. She sounded more curious than alarmed, and Rex explained that he had heard about a young couple looking at Ernest Blackwell's property and wanted to know if such a couple had been shown hers.

"Maybe," she said with a teasing twinkle in her eyes. "You'd better come in out of the damp." She unhooked the chain and opened the door wide. "My bronchitis acts up in this climate. That's why I've decided to move." She closed the door behind them and gestured to her right. "Go on in," she invited and followed the two men into a living room where a central ceiling lamp reflected the comforting glow through the window. The decor in tan and peach hues was soothing on the eyes. "My husband will be back any minute," she added.

Rex had already noticed she didn't wear an engagement ring or a wedding band. Nor did any photos of nuptials or children adorn the tables or shelves.

She perched on an armchair opposite a sofa and waited for her visitors to take a seat. Although her wavy hair was loose about her shoulders, she was dressed in business attire comprising black slacks and an expensive-looking sweater in a sludgy green that set off her eyes. A pair of high heels lay discarded by the sofa. Through her nylons peeped bright red toenails. She tossed back her dark curls, sending a pair of silver hoops bobbing and glinting in her ears.

"So," she said, clasping her hands, "why the interest in a young couple looking at Mr. Blackwell's property?"

"Lottie Green mentioned them as potential buyers for his house," Malcolm said while Rex continued to mull over the contradiction of a married woman without a ring.

"Not now, surely?" she asked. "I mean, it's a crime scene. Who'd want to buy a house where two violent murders have been committed?"

"Ghouls," Rex said.

She smiled.

"You know Lottie?" Malcolm asked.

"I know of her. I don't have much to do with the neighbours. I run a business from home and I'm often away for meetings."

"What do you do?" Malcolm wanted to know.

"I have a travel website called Get Up and Go. It's geared towards last-minute deals for spontaneous travellers. I go out and solicit sponsors and advertisers."

"Well, anyhow," Malcolm went on to Rex's amusement. Usually his friend wasn't so assertive. "We were keen to find out if this couple had been here and whether you could tell us anything about them." He glanced at Rex to see how he was doing, and Rex nodded in approval.

"Okay," the woman said in a hesitant voice. "But I still don't see what they have to do with the murders. Are you working with the police?"

"I am," Malcolm replied. "I'm a forensic medical examiner by profession. I went to the station today with additional information, and now this other bit of news has turned up. This couple may know something. We'd like to talk to them. Rex here is really the brains of the team."

"I should have introduced myself," she said, turning her attention to Rex and smiling wide enough to produce two charming dimples. "Charlotte Spelling. And my husband won't be turning up. I don't have one. Anymore. I just said that before because I didn't know who you both were, and I was acting out of precaution."

"I understand," Rex said.

"Okay, well, I don't know what you need to know exactly, but a young couple did come by to see my house. They wanted a quiet neighbourhood and so were looking in Notting Hamlet. They saw my For Sale sign and rang the doorbell on spec."

"Can you describe them?" Malcolm asked.

"A nice-looking couple. She was quite stunning, actually. Blonde, medium height. John and Mary Jones, they said their names were."

"You said 'they said their names were,'" Rex queried, picking up on the fact that Charlotte Spelling had not simply stated their names.

She flashed him a look, her gaze lingering on him for a second. "Right. They didn't sound like a John and Mary Jones."

"How so?"

"I'm not sure, but they sounded Romanian or Russian—something like that. It wasn't immediately noticeable, and his accent was rather heavier than hers. He had broad features and cold dark eyes that really stood out in his pasty complexion. He gave me the chills, actually."

"You are very observant, Miss Spelling," Rex complimented.

"You can call me Charlie. My friends do."

Malcolm raised an eyebrow at Rex, which Rex chose to ignore. "Did they spend long looking around?"

"Yes, quite awhile. Mostly he paced around upstairs and down, while she asked questions about the neighbourhood. What were the neighbours like? What did they do? Was it safe and quiet? I told her it was for the most part. But I didn't get the impression this couple would fit in that well. They looked like they should be living in some yuppie suburb. Her, anyway. I don't know if her diamonds were real, but they looked it, and she was wrapped in white fur, and wore white suede ankle-length boots. White! Hardly practical."

"And the man?"

"Heavy overcoat, leather gloves."

Rex nodded as he took down notes in his pad. "Did they say if they liked the house?"

"They said it was lovely, but after all the looking around and opening cupboards, they said they needed four bedrooms because they planned to start a family."

"A large family," Rex suggested, and was again rewarded with a smile.

Malcolm coughed. "And you never heard from them again?"

"No." Charlotte shrugged in defeat. "I just got their names. But I'll tell you what else was odd..."

Rex leaned attentively across the coffee table. "Go on."

"Well, the next day I ran into Ernest Blackwell at the greengrocer's in Godminton. I asked if he was having any luck selling his house, because I wasn't. And he said that only the day before he'd had a young couple from Argentina who were very interested and said they'd be back. Well, you don't get many young couples around here, but age is relative, so to an old man like Ernest anyone below forty-five would be young. My couple were in their early thirties. And I thought I might have mistaken the accent. So I asked him what they looked like, just to be sure, and it was them! The broad-shouldered bloke, the beautiful blonde in the white fur. You could tell Ernest was quite smitten. But what got me was the fact they had said they were looking for four bedrooms, and Ernest has the exact same floor plan as me, the Elm. Only the Oak has four bedrooms."

"I have the Oak," Malcolm put in with a modest cough. "Most of the homes on Badger Court are Oaks."

"Perhaps they liked the fact that Ernest's house backs onto woods," Rex pointed out.

"It's possible. But, all put together, it seemed strange. I mean, for one thing, she didn't look like she was from Argentina. And him, apart from the hair and eyes? I don't think so."

"The world had become a very migratory place," Malcolm opined. "Even the UK."

Rex was well acquainted with his friend's conservative views, which were hardly relevant to the inquiry. "But Ernest appeared to have no such suspicions?" he asked Charlotte.

"No, he just seemed happy to have a potential buyer. I've had no bites. Even less likely to now," she said ruefully.

"How was Chris Walker as a house agent?" Rex asked.

"Pleasant enough. I've never had any issues with him. Who would have thought?" Charlotte hugged her arms and shook her dark locks. "The times he sat on that sofa where you're seated..." she said, pointing her head in the men's direction. "Doesn't really bear thinking about. I'd like to switch agents, but I have an agreement with the firm. In any case, it's not like Chris Walker's been convicted, is it?"

"Innocent until proven guilty," Rex said.

"But, in a way, I hope it's him. Otherwise it means the killer is still at large, and I might be next!" The colour drained from Charlotte's face. "That's if it's true only sellers are being targeted. What if it's some crazy person in Notting Hamlet who doesn't want anybody to leave?"

"If the police are interested in Chris Walker, there's probably good reason," Malcolm attempted to reassure her.

"But why? Why would he murder four of his clients? It doesn't make sense!"

Rex had to agree, but he kept quiet. Presumably, the police were equipped with more information than they had released to Malcolm. "Do you know a handyman by the name of Randy?" he asked Charlotte.

"Handy Randy?" She almost laughed. "I've seen him about the neighbourhood. He drives by and leers at me from his van. He thinks he's God's gift. Why do you ask?"

"I understand he did odd jobs for the four victims."

"Oh, I see." She looked pensive—and worried. "Do you think I'm in danger?"

"Are you all alone here?" Malcolm asked solicitously.

"Well … yes. I've thought about going to stay with a friend, but it's difficult when my home office is here."

"Do you at least have secure locks? An alarm?" Malcolm asked.

Charlotte nodded, and made a visible effort to cover her panic. "Listen, can I offer either of you anything to drink? Tea, coffee, Scottish malt?" she asked Rex.

Tempted as he was by the whisky and the mellow ambience of the room, he declined, and Malcolm followed suit.

"We've probably taken up enough of your time," Rex said warmly and stood up. Malcolm did likewise, though more reluctantly. Rex shook Charlotte's hand at the front door and expressed his thanks for her helpfulness and hospitality.

"You will let me know if you come up with anything?" she asked.

"Most assuredly."

She opened the door, fitted with a Chubb lock and the thick safety chain, and the men huddled into their coats against the damp cold. Rex turned on the path to bid Charlotte goodbye again before she closed the door.

"Why did you refuse a drink?" Malcolm asked, clearly disgruntled, as the two men made their way down the driveway.

"I felt bad aboot accepting her hospitality when we're not here in an official capacity, as you intimated."

"I did not."

"You said you were the forensic medical examiner."

"I said I was *an* FME," Malcolm corrected him.

"You implied you were *the* FME. And you're really a forensic pathologist."

"I didn't want to scare her off."

"You wanted to impress her?"

"Well, dealing only with dead bodies is not generally considered glamorous."

Amused, Rex pulled his friend's arm in the direction of the cul-de-sacs. "Let's try the third 'For Sale.'" This was the only property listed under a different real estate broker than Walker & Associates. "Then we'll go for some pub grub."

"And a drink," Malcolm approved, trotting after him. "Ever since Charlie mentioned booze, I've had a craving. It'll help chase away the chill."

Rex duly noted the "Charlie" and smiled to himself. "Do you know the sellers on Otter Court?" he asked.

"The Ballantines. Rick and Sandra, and their teenage son. Name's Will, I think. Don't see him about much. He's a bit of a loner. Likes to stay inside playing video games, especially the violent ones, according to his mother."

"I might have seen him this morning, heading through the green towards the river. A pale, lanky lad, with an unruly mop of chestnut hair?

"That's him."

The sign in the front yard of the Ballantine house, which stood on a pie-shaped lot towards the end of the cul-de-sac, depicted two interlocking silver triangles. The name EuroConnect was printed in bold letters beneath. Rex pressed the doorbell, but no one answered the chime.

He knocked once, twice. "Nobody's home," he said, conceding defeat. "I'd like to know if the foreign couple swung by here. This is a four-bedroom, by the looks of it."

"Yes, it's an Oak. You can tell by the dormer window. I think that's Will's bedroom. I often see his light on late at night."

Rex didn't think of his friend as a night owl, yet refrained from asking what he was often doing out late. Malcolm was a grown man, and it was better than thinking of him spending all his evenings in with TV dinners. Rex gazed up at the dormer window and pictured the teenager alone in his room intent on his video games. His own son had been more into sports and girls at that age. He'd been an only child, too. Rex decided to call Campbell that evening and see how things were going with his graduate studies and life in general.

"The Ballantines are moving so Will can be closer to kids his age and, hopefully, integrate better," Malcolm informed him as they walked back to Badger Court. "There aren't many teenagers here." A light drizzle began to fall and they popped open their umbrellas.

"You said 'integrate.' Antisocial tendencies?" Rex asked.

"Maybe not 'anti,' but none. I've never heard more than a mumbled 'hello' from the lad. And you can barely see him through all that hair falling into his face. Grungy is the word I'd use to describe his appearance. I pity his parents, really."

"It could be a passing phase," Rex said as they entered Malcolm's driveway. "Take my car to the pub?" he asked his friend.

"Fine. I'll navigate."

"You'll have to. I don't want to get lost again. You can point oot the signs that should be there." In this godforsaken place, he almost added.

EIGHT

Installed in a booth at the King's Head with their pints and shepherd's pie, Rex listened as Malcolm remarked how good it felt to be away from Notting Hamlet for a spell enjoying a late lunch. Rex had to agree. He found the community depressing, though whether more from the serial murders or the dismal weather, he could not be sure. A fire blazed in the hearth and horse brasses and old photographs of local scenic spots covered the walls, providing a genial atmosphere of welcome and warmth.

"So, to recap," Rex said looking around the lounge to ensure no one was within earshot, "the estate agent is as of now the main police suspect and we have discovered the existence of a pair of foreigners who might be posing as homebuyers."

"Perhaps they have nothing better to do than dress up and go looking at property they can't afford. Bet you a second pint the fur and diamonds are fake."

"Let's see if we can learn anything from the sales office."

On the way to the pub, they had driven past Chris Walker's premises on the High Street in Godminton, a small market town of old and the closest to Notting Hamlet.

"And I'd like to try the Ballantine house again when we get back."

"Or we could just phone. I have Rick's number somewhere," Malcolm said. "I wonder why they went with a different estate agent," he added, a forkful of cheesy mashed potato poised before his lips.

"Would you retain the services of a house agent whose properties have been the scenes of four grisly murders?"

"I suppose not." Malcolm put the food in his mouth and chewed thoughtfully. "Though Walker hadn't been arrested then." He swallowed and washed down the potato with his pint of bitter.

"He hasn't been arrested at all as far as we know," Rex pointed out. "His name hasn't even been released to the media. We only have it on hearsay that it's him the police are interested in."

"I had it confirmed this morning," Malcolm reminded him. "When DCI Cooper told me about the wet shoeprint on the mat. Perhaps his name will be on the evening news." He swiped the paper napkin across his mouth with relish.

Clearly, Malcolm didn't want the police releasing Walker and detaining him instead on the basis of the destroyed blood evidence. "Even so," Rex said, getting back to the Ballantines. "I wonder how much Rick and Sandra's motivation to move was prompted by the murders. You said they'd been wanting to find a different environment or special care for their son?"

"Will is not special needs, exactly," Malcolm said. "It's just a bit isolating for him in the Hamlet. No kids of his age."

Rex had not seen many of the residents, but from what Malcolm had told him, the demographic seemed stagnant: a lot of retirees, and not many young commuters or entrepreneurs working from home. Families with small children were few and far between. Until the epidemic of selling fever, there had not been much transition in the community. No new blood, as Malcolm had put it.

"You mentioned some undesirable people in Notting Hamlet," Rex said, reaching for his Guinness. "I want to get as complete a picture as I can of the community."

"Yes, along Owl Lane, running parallel to Notting Hamlet Road. Three of the houses have a least one motorcycle. The owners are always tinkering with them, parts and accessories littering the driveways. Quite unsightly, really. As are the owners."

"How do you mean, exactly?" asked Rex, who had a soft spot for bikers since being involved in a murder investigation in Key West.

Malcolm shook his head censoriously. "Scraggly hair, tattoos, which are mostly covered up in this weather, mercifully. Some of the designs are downright offensive. And most of them don't look like they've bathed in weeks," he muttered in distaste. "They drink beer in one or other of their driveways or in the garage when it's raining and jeer at the passers-by."

Rex listened to Malcolm's tirade with mild amusement while he finished the remnants of his pie. "Lowers the tone," he remarked with a sardonic smile.

"Too right it does! You have to go through the street to get in and out. No avoiding it. I suppose it's a blessing they're down by the entrance where most of us can't hear them revving their engines, but sometimes they swarm around the neighbourhood on their rigs, scaring the living daylight out of the residents."

"Do these people work?" Rex asked.

Malcolm almost choked on his bitter. "Not that you'd notice. Most of them aren't *gainfully* employed. I suspect they deal. Weed," he whispered, his eyes swivelling around the lounge, although the only clientele sat at the bar and at one of the end booths. "Don't mention to anyone I told you this," he said nervously. "I don't want to end up dead."

"You mean, like Ernest Blackwell and the others?"

Malcolm stared at him. "You know, I never seriously considered them in connection with the murders."

"Why not?"

Malcolm scratched the back of his grey head. "Garrotting, carbon monoxide poisoning, electrocution ..."

"Quite the repertoire, isn't it?"

"Yes, indeed. Sort of sophisticated in a macabre sort of way. And no prints."

"You don't associate that level of professionalism with your biker friends?"

Malcolm shook his head, hesitantly at first, then more vigorously. "No, I just can't see it. Except for the bludgeoning."

"But if they tinker all day long with their bikes, they're probably pretty handy in all sorts of ways."

"I suppose."

The server came by to sweep up their empty plates and asked if they wanted dessert. Upon Malcolm's request, she listed the puddings. Rex, resolved to order only a coffee, felt his willpower give way at the mention of treacle tart.

"And I'll have the banana split," Malcolm ordered. "Everything is homemade here," he told Rex, as though in justification of their lack of self-discipline.

"Who would the bikers sell to?" Rex asked when the young girl had left their table. "Not to a community of retirees, surely?"

Malcolm thought for a moment. "They may have customers within the community or else further afield. I don't know everybody in the Hamlet. There are about a hundred and fifty residents, not all of them retired. And then there are the outlying villages and Godminton." He gave Rex an overview of the area.

"Aye, it's isolated enough around here for them to grow their product under minimum security."

"Until the police swooped in to investigate the murders," Malcolm pointed out. He coughed in warning as the server approached and placed their desserts before them.

"Thanks, lass," Rex said, looking in appreciation at the gooey treacle on pastry and the small jug of custard.

"Pretty little thing, isn't she?" Malcolm said, staring after her before tucking into his pudding.

"They're all pretty at that age," Rex said, "or at least know how to make themselves so."

"That Charlotte was charming, I thought." His friend scooped up a spoonful of banana and ice cream. "Took a fancy to you," he added when he received no comment from Rex.

"Aside from the fact I'm engaged to a woman who is perfection personified, I make it a habit not to let charm blind or bedazzle me in an investigation."

"Weren't you supposed to be married in the spring?" Malcolm asked.

"That was the plan. But it came around so fast we decided to postpone until we were less busy. Helen wants a big wedding. It's her first and she wants it to be perfect. It's going to require a lot of organization."

Malcolm nodded. "It's difficult when you're both working and live in different parts of the UK."

"Aye, but we make it work." Rex set down his spoon. "Why don't you pursue the charming Charlotte? She's divorced and you're a widower. It's been three years. Charlotte might have flirted with you had you been the one not wearing a wedding ring."

His friend twisted the gold band on his finger. "Not sure I'm ready to move on yet. How long was it before you got over Fiona?"

Rex sighed heavily. "It was a long time," he conceded. He had lost his wife to breast cancer when his son was fifteen. It had been an excruciating period in their lives.

"But now you have Helen," Malcolm said on a more cheerful note.

"And we have four murders to solve," Rex said in like vein, throwing down his napkin and looking around for the server so they could settle their bill. It was time to call on Walker's office and see what they could find out about the mysterious couple who had expressed interest in the property belonging to the late Ernest Blackwell.

NINE

REX MANAGED TO FIND on-street parking in front of the firm owned by Chris Walker. Photos of properties surmounted by brief descriptions lined the window. None, he noted, were located in Notting Hamlet. Those must have been taken down. In a bare space in the glass, he saw the blurry reflection of a solidly built man with reddish hair and beard, his neck swaddled in a scarf. He blinked at his image and caught Malcolm's beside him, greyer, thinner, and shorter. A lot of time had passed since their university days.

The door chimed brightly as they entered. Behind a partition at the far end of the office bobbed the heads of a couple of people whom Rex took to be sales associates. From a reception desk angled in the narrow space in the foreground, a buxom bleached blonde enquired in an ingratiating voice whether she could be of assistance. Her nametag, pinned to a ruffled crimson silk blouse, read "Lea."

"I hope so," Rex replied with what he hoped was his most amiable smile. "It's regarding the homes for sale in Notting Hamlet."

The woman's face darkened around her creased blue eyeshadow. "Are you reporters?" she demanded, casting a look at Malcolm. Her hand reached for the desk phone.

"No, nothing like that," Rex assured her, assessing the lay of the land. He surmised the office had been besieged by the media and nosy members of the public in weeks past. "I'm trying to locate my daughter." This was the story he had concocted with Malcolm on the way to Chris Walker's premises in the event they encountered resistance, a story designed to elicit sympathy and the most information possible. Rex's inherently honest nature rebelled at resorting to subterfuge, but an innocent man's freedom might be at stake and he had to help his friend out of a legal jam.

"I don't see how I can assist you there," the receptionist said in a relenting tone, her assumed one of formality failing to disguise her broad country dialect. Then, unable to contain her curiosity, she asked, "Is she missing then? I have an adult daughter myself."

"Aye," Rex said, sighing deeply into his muffler. "The police won't help us because she's of age, but she took up with an undesirable character and I need to get her back home before she throws her life away. This is my old friend Malcolm, who's kindly helping me."

Malcolm stood by, looking grave.

"But what does this have to do with Notting Hamlet?" the woman asked.

The ceaseless chatter and activity behind the partition led Rex to wonder whether the agents were packing up now that their employer was a prime suspect in a case where four stigmatized properties were listed under his name.

"Closing up shop?" he asked the receptionist.

"Reorganizing."

He would have liked to ask after Chris Walker but her demeanour, which had reverted to guarded, warned him to stick to his story. "We tracked my daughter from Edinburgh to Bedford, and we understand they were going to settle down in the area. When we were asking around Notting Hamlet, a resident told us she had seen a young woman fitting my daughter's description in the company of the individual we want to save her from. This was around three weeks ago." Rex hoped his blend of fact and fiction sounded convincing. "We decided to try here when we saw your For Sale signs in the neighbourhood, in case she'd come in." He gave Lea a pleading look, parent to parent.

"Do you have a photo?" she asked. "I never forget a face."

Rex had not had time to prepare for this eventuality. He turned to Malcolm. "You have it."

"Do I?" Malcolm patted down his pockets both inside and outside his raincoat. He began to look frantic. "I'm sorry, Rex. I think I must've left it at the pub when we were asking the staff if they'd seen her. The waitress took it to the landlord to see if he'd served the couple at the bar."

"We'll have to go back for it." Rex stared reprovingly at Malcolm, but inwardly applauded his quick thinking and consummate acting skills. "She's an attractive blonde, five foot-six, stylish in her dress," he told the receptionist, attempting to compensate for failing to produce a photograph. "She may be using a false identity and trying to disguise her Scottish accent. Her real name is Amanda Graves. He's dark-haired and dark-eyed, powerfully built, and he's definitely foreign."

Lea brushed her blatantly painted fingertips across the desk. "You do know what happened in Notting Hamlet?" she asked, looking up at Rex with a mixture of fear and concern.

"The murders. I know. That's why we're doubly anxious."

"I'm surprised the police didn't want to help you, considering," Lea said astutely, leaving the statement hanging in the air.

Rex continued to recount his story in an attempt to distract her from this obvious point. Any visitor to Notting Hamlet at the time of the murders should have aroused police interest. "We have reason to believe my daughter and this man were interested in purchasing a property on Fox Lane. They were going by the names of Mary and John Jones."

"Not very original," the receptionist opined.

"No, indeed. We were wondering if they might have left a forwarding address or phone number."

"I don't recall them, and, in any case, I'm not supposed to give out such information," the receptionist demurred, not without a hint of apology.

"These are special circumstances. Could you please—please!— check for their names in your system? You may be our only hope," Rex said, appealing to the compassionate nature he discerned the woman possessed.

Expelling a sigh, she tapped the keys of her computer and spent some minutes reviewing the information on the screen, while Rex and Malcolm exchanged wondering glances. "I have a record of four couples and one man who viewed Fox Lane properties," Lea said, glancing up at the men. "We have four properties on that street."

Woods, Spelling, Trotter, and Blackwell, Rex recounted to himself. "The house belonging to a Mr. Ernest Blackwell is the one my daughter appeared to favour," Rex supplied to make sure they were talking about the same property.

"Ernest Blackwell, deceased."

"Right. Naturally, I'm even more concerned for my daughter's safety now." Rex watched anxiously as Lea screwed up her eyes once more and scanned the screen.

"There's no John and Mary Jones anywhere here," she said. "They could have just walked in off the street without making an appointment. There's a note here saying Mr. Blackwell called to say a couple were interested in his home and he'd referred them to Chris. He hadn't managed to get their number and the name he gave was Juan and Maria Garcia."

"John and Mary in Spanish," Malcolm said. "And another common surname."

"Who entered that information on the prospect into your system?" Rex asked.

"Chris Walker. The entry is dated the fourth of November. That's right before the murders. There's no follow-up. Not much Chris could do without any contact information. Why would your daughter and her boyfriend use a false name and pose as a married couple?"

"We pray they're not married," Malcolm said, with feeling. "Presumably they're using aliases because they don't want to be found."

"They'd need to use their legal names to enter into a valid house contract," Rex said. "Maybe they weren't as interested as they said."

"They'd do better renting if they want to stay anonymous," Lea remarked. "I'm sorry I can't help you further. I only met a few of these couples, and none of them were young, exactly. How old is your daughter?"

"Thirty," Rex lied. That was the approximate age Charlotte Spelling had given, though it seemed a bit old for a father to be chasing after his errant daughter. "She's very naïve and impressionable," he added.

"You must have had her young," Lea noted, contemplating him with compassion. "No, these other couples were older. Forties, fifties, at least." She sat back in her swivel chair with an air of defeat. "I wish I could've been of more help. I do hope you find her."

"Thank you," Rex said. "And I really appreciate your time." He produced his card from his wallet and handed it to her. "In case you remember anything more ..."

"Oh, you're a QC." Lea was clearly impressed. "Not that it would do Chris any good since you're a Scottish barrister."

"Has Mr. Walker sought counsel?" Rex asked, seeing an opening for information on the suspect.

"I don't know. But it probably doesn't matter how good his representation is, since he doesn't have much of a defence. He admitted to being at Mr. Blackwell's house the day of the murders. No point in denying it. His car was parked outside for the whole street to see. What's more," Lea added, leaning forward in her chair, "he was charged with a drunk and disorderly when he was at university. I know that much because my nephew's with the Bedfordshire Police. And," she emphasized, looking behind her to make sure she wasn't overheard, "Chris's ex-wife took out a restraining order against him—said he was verbally abusive and attacked her on one occasion. But she's a right little madam. Once he started making money in this business, she was always demanding more."

It occurred to Rex that Lea seemed to know a lot about Chris Walker's personal life, though whether more from her nephew or Walker's own mouth he could only speculate. Significantly, however, not once had she referred to him as Mr. Walker.

"Have you spoken to your employer since he was taken in for questioning?" he asked.

"I haven't. And that's a bad sign. Ever since the murders, he's been busy trying to save the business and going out of his mind with stress, and not getting any sleep. He looked like death warmed up even before the police were interested in him as a suspect." Lea closed her blue lids and shook her head. "I dread to think what state he's in now. In fact, I can't believe this is happening at all!"

"Nothing's happened yet," Rex said. "It might not look good for your employer, but from here to court is a long way off."

"My lawyer friend should know," Malcolm put in with a grave nod. "It must be a shock for you. Do you believe he's innocent?"

Lea gazed at him vacantly. "I do, deep down. But I'll admit there are moments I have my doubts. I mean, you never want to believe it of someone close, do you?"

Rex sighed in sympathy. "Aye, well, all the best to you." He held out his hand and squeezed hers warmly. He and Malcolm left in silence and regained the car parked out front.

"Didn't get much," Malcolm said, standing on the damp street decorated with Christmas lights and tinsel stars and stockings that did nothing to cheer the gloomy aspect of the aging buildings and leaden grey sky. "Except that now we know Walker has a history of violence."

Rex agreed as he got in his car, but mostly with Malcolm's first statement—that they had not learnt much. Lots of people got drunk and disorderly in college and even went on to abuse their spouse, but few ended up going on killing sprees. "It might be worth looking into any unsolved local murders," he suggested. "If Walker is our man, he may have escalated from the charges on record before graduating to serial murder."

"Good point," Malcolm said, settling in the passenger seat. "And interesting about the foreign couple's name change, don't you think?"

"Aye, but we're no closer to discovering who they are." Rex turned the ignition and prepared to manoeuvre out of the small space.

"And no tie-in with the letters on the victims, except for Mary or Maria. But names beginning with 'M' are common. Not Malcolm so much, but Mark or Michael."

Rex glanced over at his friend, who sounded agitated. "Relax," he said.

"Easy for you to say. It's not your initials that were written on the bodies. What is your middle name, anyway?"

"Clarence."

"Really? I never knew that."

"I don't make it public knowledge."

"Quite." Malcolm gave a discreet cough. "Interesting, as well, that the couple were acting on their own and didn't go through Chris Walker's office," he said, tactfully changing topic. "Since he never spoke with them, the only eyewitnesses we know of are Charlotte and Ernest, who's dead."

Rex let his friend's comment loom in the air as they drove down the street. Was Charlotte Spelling, the other known witness, at risk?

TEN

"So, what now, Sherlock?" Malcolm asked Rex from the passenger seat.

"I'd like to try the Ballantines again, for starters."

"I think their house went up for sale after the murders," Malcolm reminded him. "You think the foreign couple went back to Notting Hamlet after that?"

"You never know."

"We should probably pick up something for dinner while we're here, unless you want frozen again. There's a Sainsbury's on the outskirts of Godminton." Malcolm gave Rex directions. After a moment, he spoke again. "I remember there was a murder here almost four years ago that never got solved. A single mother of two who'd just moved to town. I did the autopsy. She'd been strangled, most likely by a neck tie or similar item, judging from the indentation mark on her flesh." He sighed wistfully. "Lovely bone structure. Such a shame."

"She'd just moved here?" Rex asked, taking the turn Malcolm indicated.

"Yes. There was no sign of a break-in, nothing stolen. The police tried to pin her murder on her ex, a foreign national, as I recall, but they never made it stick. Yvonne Callister." Malcolm drew out the name as though it had just come back to him. "I think he might have been a Cypriot or a Spaniard. He ultimately got the children. They attended the local primary school over there."

"You seem to remember a lot," Rex remarked, glancing across at his friend.

"Well, some cases just stay with you. She was only in her mid-thirties, and for the two young ones to lose their mother in such a tragic way..."

"What I'm thinking," Rex said, pulling into the parking lot of the Sainsbury's supermarket, "is that she must have rented or bought her house from someone. And that someone might just conceivably have been Chris Walker, especially as the home murder fits the *modus operandi*."

"Oh, yes, I see. I'll find out, shall I? And I'll dig into other cold cases around here, as well."

"Grand. Well, let's get to it," Rex said, stepping out of the car. Shopping was not high on his list of favourite activities, but another frozen dinner did not appeal any more than Malcolm's nondescript brand of coffee.

The two bachelors grabbed a cart and proceeded down the extensive aisles of packaged goods. It soon became apparent they employed radically different strategies for procuring items. Malcolm methodically rooted around the stacked shelves for the economically priced brands his late wife had preferred. "Jocelyn always got this," he kept saying.

Rex, who lived with his mother when not at his Highlands retreat, was not a savvy shopper and pretty much threw whatever he fancied into the cart, much to Malcolm's growing dismay. Rex told his friend the groceries were on him and he didn't want to spend the rest of the afternoon at the store.

"But you can't pay for all this," Malcolm said ogling the bottles of Sainsbury's label wine, gourmet cold meats and cheeses, and pricey ready-prepared food.

"Nonsense. My treat."

"But I invited you down, and you're being kind enough to help me out."

"You paid for lunch. Now let's get this stuff rung up so we can get oot of here." Rex pushed off with the cart, leaving Malcolm to follow, uttering protestations.

By the time they reached the parking lot, the afternoon had darkened to dusk and the lamps had come on, helping them circumvent the puddles. Above the diffused brightness of the lights, black clouds scudded across the sky, but failed to chase away the rain that had started again when the men were in the store. The ominous weather only seemed to portend more misfortune.

The drive took longer on the way back to Notting Hamlet due to the rainfall. The lanes winding around the dripping hedgerows proved slippery and treacherous, and the car skidded a few times in the mud. The wipers sluiced the windshield while the downpour continued to shower the cottony landscape of flat fields and copses on either side of the road.

"You said Handy Randy lived on Owl Lane?"

"We're not stopping there, are we?" Malcolm asked in shock.

"Why not? He did work on all four victims' homes. It's a coincidence worth looking into."

"He's worked on many homes in the Hamlet," Malcolm countered. "He's the resident handyman. And the police eliminated him from their inquiries."

"But he knew the victims. He may be able to provide some insight. And since we have decided to meddle in this case, for better or worse," Rex said, looking over at Malcolm, "I think we should call on him. There's no point in approaching this half-cocked."

"What about the shopping?"

"It won't spoil in the boot, will it? Not in this temperature."

Having run out of objections, Malcolm fell quiet. He seemed uneasy as they approached the ungated entrance to Notting Hamlet, shifting in his seat and sitting more upright. Rex felt sure, if his friend had been driving, he would not have turned onto Owl Lane.

"Left or right?" Rex asked.

"Left," Malcolm said with obvious reluctance. "I really don't feel safe on this street." He stared out his window at the mock-Tudor homes, which were architecturally identical to those in the rest of the community, yet more neglected in appearance. Overturned trash bins and appliances discarded on the curb promoted the impression of an inferior neighbourhood.

"It's this one." Malcolm pointed through the passenger window.

Randall's property was the best-maintained Rex had seen on Owl Lane. He took in the recently painted window frames and gutters free of leaves and debris, as befitted a jack-of-all-trades. A swing set stood on the tidy lawn beside a small kennel painted green, but, in spite of the fact the rain had eased off, he saw neither child nor dog.

They left the car on the street and walked up the cobble-paved path. Rex knocked firmly at the familiar four-panelled hardwood door with central iron knob. He had faced many such doors in the community. He did not have long to wait.

The door swung inwards to reveal a blondish woman in baggy sweatpants holding a runny-nosed toddler against her stained sweater. She looked impatient and suspicious at the same time.

"Sorry to bother you," Rex said. "Is your husband home?" Not knowing Randall's last name, he felt it best to refer to him in this manner. The woman looked about the right age to be his wife, though her appearance was by no means up to the level of her property, her dark inch-long roots and peeling nail polish in dire need of a touch-up.

"He's on a job," she replied in a coarse voice. "What do you want him for?" She eyed the men more suspiciously still.

"I was thinking of remodelling my kitchen," Malcolm said. "I live on Badger Court, number Sixty-One. The name's Malcolm Patterson. I'm in the book."

The toddler began squirming and fussing in the woman's arms. His chin began to crumple up even as Rex watched. From cherubic lips ensued a stuttering whine, precursor to a full-blown tantrum.

"I'll tell him." The prospect of a big job rendered the woman's tone more agreeable. "Oh, I won't have to. There he is now." She jerked her unmade face toward the street, where an older-model grey panel van was turning into the driveway. On its side a decal advertised "Good-as-New Home Maintenance" and gave a phone number. The child started waving his arms energetically and uttering a series of shrieks.

Rex thanked the woman, turned from the doorstep, and headed towards the van, Malcolm in tow.

"Remodelling your kitchen, eh?" he asked his friend in a low voice, smiling at his deception.

"Thinking of," Malcolm qualified.

The driver of the van, a man pushing fifty, rolled down his window and leaned out to greet them. "Randall Gomez at your service," he said, nodding a greeting.

Rex guessed the uniformly jet-black hair was helped along with a little dye. Jaunty blue eyes stood out from the man's olive skin, which was beginning to sag at the jawline and fold at the base of the neck where a plaited gold chain nestled in the flesh. A self-rolled cigarette hung limp between the fore and middle fingers of his right hand, now resting on the van's windowsill. He got out and stood before the two visitors.

Malcolm reached out his hand and introduced himself. "I was thinking of putting in a new kitchen. I gave your wife my particulars." The woman in question had taken the screaming child back into the house and closed the door. "I heard you'd done some work for Ernest Blackwell and others in the neighbourhood, and wondered if you might be able to provide some references."

"You won't get a reference from Ernest any more than I'll get my pay cheque. He's dead, mate. Don't you watch the news?"

Malcolm pursed his lips before speaking. "Of course I do. I take it you didn't get paid?"

"Oh, he was good for it, was old Ernest. Never forgot stuff like that, but his death was what you might call untimely. I'd all but completed a plumbing job for him, and next thing I knew someone had done the poor geezer in with piano wire. He loved all those music hall tunes, did Ernest. He'd be playing them while I worked. He'd always make me a cup of tea and we'd have a good old natter. He was partial to Jaffa cakes; I suppose because the sponge and orange jam was easy on his dentures." Randall stroked away a tear from the corner of his eye. "Poor old bugger. Didn't deserve that."

"I'm sure the others didn't either," Rex said with a commiserating sigh. "Did you know them well?"

"Vic and Barry? Well enough. Barry was a character, too. Hard to have a conversation with, though, on account of his hearing aid. I kept telling him he needed a new one. I didn't do much work for Vic Chandler. He could fix most stuff himself, but he didn't have a head for heights and wouldn't go up a ladder. That's when he'd call me. I put up his satellite dish."

Rex felt Malcolm bristle beside him.

"And Valerie Trotter?" Rex enquired.

"What about her?" Randy asked defiantly. The man took a long pull of his rollie.

"My friend's been following the case," Malcolm said on Rex's behalf. "He didn't mean to speak out of turn."

"Right, well, about this job you want doing," the handyman said. "I could come round and give you an estimate, bring some samples. I did Vera Murdock's on Fox Lane. Came out lovely," he said with a cocky air. "She'll give you a reference all right."

"Terrific." Malcolm gave Randall Gomez his phone number and suggested he come by early the following week.

The two men got back in their car as Randall stood by, watching.

"Not sure he believed you," Rex told Malcolm as he made a U-turn on the street.

"Well, I hope you're satisfied. I told you it would be a waste of time."

"Maybe," Rex said.

"I don't trust that chap, or his slattern of a wife."

"Och, she wasna that bad!" Rex retorted in Scots vernacular, as he often did when indignant. "She probably does not get much time to herself what with a wee bairn and two other children."

"You wouldn't find their sort in Morningside," his friend replied snobbily, referring to Rex's genteel neighbourhood in Edinburgh.

"That's as maybe. Well, let's stop by the Ballantines', see if they're home yet."

However, as they approached the two-story home in Otter Court, no lights were visible, contrary to what one would expect on such a dull autumn afternoon had someone been home. Leaving Malcolm in the car, Rex hurried up the path to the door and rang the bell, which chimed deep within the house, the high note followed by a lower, more resonant tone. He imagined the empty air surrounding the bereft furniture and abandoned spaces waiting for the family to bring the rooms back to life.

He waited a moment longer and rapped with the iron knocker. Only the dead silence responded.

———

"I expect they're still at work," Malcolm said as Rex ducked into the car beside him.

"I was hoping the lad would be back from school. Does he drive?"

"Probably, but I don't know if he has a car. I don't come into this cul-de-sac very often. I sometimes see his upstairs light when I turn into mine."

"What do the parents do?" Rex asked, driving back to Malcolm's house.

"I think she's a teacher. Rick's an accountant, commutes to Bedford. That may be another reason for wanting to move, so he can be closer to work."

"I got their house agent's number off the sign. David Gleeson. I'll see if the house was shown to a young couple. Any chance you could call DCI Cooper and elicit some more information?" Rex had to admit he was feeling pretty stumped at this point.

"I was at the station only this morning," Malcolm objected. "It would look like I'm pestering him. And I doubt he'd tell me anything more than he already has."

Rex pulled into Malcolm's driveway and stopped the car. He sighed dispiritedly. Four corpses and little in the way of meaningful clues.

"You've only been on the case since yesterday evening," Malcolm consoled him as he unbuckled his seat belt. "We've made some headway. We now know from Chris Walker's receptionist that he has form. And we also know the young couple didn't go through his office and probably never met him. So they wouldn't be able to give us any information about him. It's not a lead, but at least we know it's a dead end. Perhaps you'll have more luck with David Gleeson."

While his friend unpacked the groceries, Rex put on the coffee, using the Colombian roast he had purchased at Sainsbury's. At least Malcolm didn't stint on the heating, and the kitchen felt nice and toasty compared to the damp cold outside.

When Malcolm went to watch the cricket on television, Rex settled at the kitchen table with his notepad, where he added Lea's and Randall Gomez's names to the list of people he had spoken to and jotted down the salient points of his and Malcolm's conversations with them. He already had Lottie Green and Charlotte Spelling. Wasn't Lottie short for Charlotte, he idly wondered? Those two residents, along with Win Prendergast, Malcolm's neighbour, and Randall were the only residents he had met so far. Mr. Woods at number 45 Fox Lane, who had slammed the door in his face, barely counted.

Next he called Gleeson, the Ballantines' house agent, and got his voicemail. As he finished leaving a message, his cell phone signalled an incoming text. It was from Helen:

Arrived safely in Miami. Recovering from jet lag but getting ready to hit South Beach and see the Art Deco. Boarding the Breeze tomorrow afternoon. So wish you could have come with us!! Julie sends her love. xxoo

Rex sent her a reply saying he had travelled to Bedfordshire for a long weekend to help out an old friend, and told her he missed her.

While TV sports commentary and civilized ripples of applause, interspersed with Malcolm's own cheering and booing, emanated from the living room, Rex transferred his attention to the newspaper crossword puzzle and had the blanks filled in within thirteen minutes according to the wall clock. Would the Ballantines be home yet? Finishing his coffee, he decided to find out, since there was little else he could do at this point.

Poking his head around the living room door, he told Malcolm he was going out and glanced long enough at the screen to note the score and the white-clad players positioned around their wickets on the green.

"Right-oh," his friend replied with a quick glance round, engrossed as he was in the cricket match. "We're winning," he crowed.

"So I see." Rex stepped back into the hall and put on his scarf. Confirming that his keys were in his pocket, he opened the door to a dark view of the front yard and driveway. A light mist sprayed his face. He reached back for his brolly. It was not far to the other cul-de-sac, and he decided to walk.

He had got as far as Barry Burn's old house when his cell phone went off in his pocket to the chorus of "The Bonnie Banks o' Loch Lomond." He paused under a streetlight and saw it was a local number. "Rex Graves," he answered, seeking shelter under a sycamore tree.

"Mr. Graves, this is David Gleeson of EuroConnect Properties returning your call."

"Thank you so much. I was calling with regard to a property in Notting Hamlet."

"The one on Otter Court?"

"Right. I wanted to know if you'd had a young foreign couple by the name of Jones or Garcia interested in it."

"No. No interest at all yet, but that's hardly surprising. I've had calls from one or two other residents in Notting Hamlet wanting to put their homes on the market, but I'm reluctant to accommodate them at this time."

"Because of the murders, no doubt," Rex said, shifting his position under the tree for better cover.

"Well, yes. I advised them to wait for the dust to settle. Plus, Notting Hamlet is largely Chris Walker's turf. I don't want to be seen as poaching his clients."

"And the Ballantine property?"

"Different kettle of fish. Rick's firm handles my finances, and I know him personally. You asked if a young couple had an interest in his house? News to me."

"An acquaintance of mine has a home listed with Chris Walker and had such a couple come by, but they seem to have vanished into thin air."

"I suppose Mr. Walker's had other things on his mind, if what I hear is true. It's a regrettable situation for his clients, but I can hardly step in and take over."

"Are you acquainted with him?" Rex asked.

"Not well. My business operates out of Bedford. We cater to a more international crowd. Perhaps you could try Covington's. They're in Godminton. It's only them and Walker now. Home Sweet Home closed its doors over a year ago."

Rex thanked Mr. Gleeson, who was beginning to sound impatient. Ending the call, he continued on his way. He felt certain he would get no more joy from Covington's. Charlotte Spelling's suspicious couple were proving impossible to trace.

ELEVEN

THE EVENLY SPACED STREETLIGHTS reflected off the puddles in the gutters, leaving pockets of darkness in between the pools of illumination. Rex pulled up his coat collar and slanted his brolly against the drizzle coming down with dreary persistence. While the knuckles of his right hand holding the brolly stem dripped water, his other was warmly ensconced in his pocket.

A few cars pulled into driveways and were swallowed by garages. Lights dotted the windows of the uniform homes he passed. Occasionally, voices and barks sounded from within, muffled by the walls and the insulating rain. He could not recall the sun having made the ghost of an appearance all day.

Once or twice, a curtain twitched and a face peered out into the gloom. He walked on and crossed into Otter Court, where the houses featured the same deep-set, small-paned windows and exposed beams across tan stucco, skirted by a brick basement. All sat in fenced-in gardens with their squares of lawn, shrubs and bushes cast in shadow. As on Badger Court, the north row backed onto the river, invisible from the street.

Rex's spirits soared when he saw the lights on downstairs at the Ballantine house, which stood at the far end of the cul-de-sac on a corner lot. A silver car was parked to one side of the driveway. At least one person was home.

He strode up to the front door and rang the bell, immediately aware of a movement in the drapes to his right. A minute later, a footfall sounded on the other side of the door, which remained resolutely closed. He held his business card in front of the peephole. The door finally opened as far as the chain would allow, and a bespectacled female face narrow in structure and framed with lank, brown hair, appeared. Her voice quavered, "Yes?"

"Mrs. Ballantine? My name is Rex Graves. Sorry to bother you when it's dark. I called on you earlier and no one was home. I'm a friend of Malcolm Patterson's on Badger Court."

"I know Dr. Patterson. The widower?"

"Correct. I wanted to ask if any people have come to view your house. Malcolm and I are conducting an independent inquiry into the murders. I spoke to your house agent, David Gleeson, just now and he said no one had expressed an interest so far, but I wondered if anyone might have come to you direct."

"With so many murders, you can see why I'm hesitant to open my door," the lady of the house explained without yet making a move to open it further.

Rex could certainly understand her reluctance and said as much. "Let me call Malcolm on my mobile, so he can vouch for me." He pulled out his phone, praying that Malcolm would not ignore his call so he could continue watching the cricket match.

"Oh, that's all right," the woman declared. "I've seen you about with him. Please come inside." She unhooked the chain and invited him into the living room. Dressed in slippers, a pleated skirt, and a buttoned cardigan, she stood with her arms folded tightly across her flat chest. Rex towered over her. "You must think me rather trusting to let a stranger into my home after what's happened," she said. "But in spite of your size, you look quite harmless."

"Thank you. I think." He smiled at the petite woman before him.

"And you're not quite a stranger, if you know Malcolm. I saw on your card that you're an officer of the law." Seemingly satisfied that he posed no danger, she said brightly, "I always treat myself to a sherry on Friday nights. Care to join me?"

"I would, thank you." Rex took a seat on the nearest armchair while she crossed to an antique buffet table and poured sherry from a decanter into two small, bell-shaped glasses.

She handed him one and sat down opposite him.

"Mrs. Ballantine—"

"Sandra."

"Sandra. You must think me very nosy coming round asking questions."

She tugged on her cultured pearl necklace. "I thought the killer's been apprehended. That other house agent ..."

"Chris Walker. I don't know that he's been arrested. Malcolm and I are just trying to get supplemental information. As you are no doubt aware, it was my friend who found the bodies."

Sandra visibly shivered as she held the sherry glass between her knees.

Rex apologized for upsetting her. "Malcolm and I were at Edinburgh University together," he elaborated. "He was studying medicine while I was getting my law degree. I occasionally get asked to investigate murder cases."

"So you're helping the police," Sandra said.

"In a manner of speaking." For all he knew, the police might construe his and Malcolm's actions as outright interference.

More at ease now, Sandra sipped her sherry and Rex did the same. It was a bit on the sweet side for his taste, but much appreciated nonetheless after his cold walk.

"You asked about visitors, but no one's come to see the house. Mr. Gleeson told us he'd had a couple of people call asking for information, but they were weeded out as having no more than a morbid curiosity. He told us to hang on."

At that moment, Rex heard the clang of the garage door, and Sandra jumped in her armchair. "That must be my husband. I wasn't expecting him so early." She looked at Rex as though working up the nerve to ask him to leave.

"Grand," he said. "I wanted to talk to him too."

A man with smarmy good looks stepped into the living room and stopped abruptly when he saw Rex. "I didn't know we had company," he said, eyeing his wife.

"This is Rex Graves, QC, a friend of Malcolm Patterson's, whom you worked with when trying to organize that automated gate for the entrance."

"I know who Malcolm is," her husband cut in. "You might perhaps have asked Mr. Graves if he wanted to remove his wet coat."

Sandra glanced at Rex in apology. "Oh, I didn't think—"

"I'm not staying long, and I'm sorry to impose." Rex turned to Mr. Ballantine, who was loosening his tie. "I was telling your wife I was interested in the Notting Hamlet murders."

"Aren't we all." Rick busied himself at the buffet table.

"Mr. Graves was asking if anyone had come to see our house, and I said no."

"Unfortunately, that's so." Her husband returned with a tumbler of liquor on the rocks. The ice rattled as he took a seat beside his wife on the sofa. Rex noted there was no physical contact between them. "I commute to Bedford practically every day," Rick Ballantine said. "It's a long haul in bad traffic. If I work late I kip on the divan at my office."

Rex noticed Sandra stiffen. I see, he thought to himself with a degree of irony. It wasn't that long of a drive.

"And we want to be closer to the city so our son can get more involved in after-school activities. It will be the same distance for my wife to travel to work. But it looks like we'll be stuck here for the time being, at least." Mr. Ballantine took a slug of his drink. "Nothing like a string of murders in a remote community to give buyers cold feet."

"Is that why you wanted to put in a gate at the front entrance?" Rex asked.

"That was before. Malcolm and I, and a few other residents, got a petition out, but a handful of homeowners resisted because of the expense. Obviously it had to be a unanimous decision, since everyone would have to be equipped with remotes or the keypad code."

"Was there some concern for safety at the time?" Rex asked.

"We were mainly thinking about break-ins. There'd been a spate of petty theft. Bicycles and tools, that sort of thing. There's a wall around the community and we thought it would be an idea to close it off completely."

"But no wall at the back, just the river," Rex said. "And not a very daunting one at that."

"True. In any event, putting a gate in now would be a bit like closing the stable door after the horse has bolted."

"It would not have impeded a menace from within the community," Rex pointed out while Sandra continued to sip at her sherry, more nervous now that her husband was home.

"Like the biker gang on Owl Lane?" Rick Ballantine asked. "There's a menace for you. It's likely they were responsible for some of the stuff going missing. They were the most vocal in opposing the gate. Wouldn't have been fair to give them access when everyone else had to chip in." Ballantine suddenly looked at his wife. "Where's Will? I didn't see his light on upstairs."

"He's with Alex."

"Alex Leontiev? You know how I feel about him hanging out with that boy."

"He's his only friend around here."

"I just don't like it." Ballantine rolled the cut-glass tumbler back and forth between his palms. "He's an Islamic militant," he told Rex. "And what are his parents doing stuck on that farm?" he asked his wife. "They barely speak English and I don't see them growing anything. One of the farms on the other side of the river," he explained to Rex.

"It's almost winter, Rick," his wife pronounced in clipped syllables.

"Can't you grow turnips in winter?" he asked. "Oh, what do I know?" Ballantine shrugged and downed the rest of his liquor. He looked as though he were contemplating a refill.

"Have you been to the farm?" Rex enquired.

"Once or twice, to collect Will. Never got out of the car. It's mucky out there and they keep a couple of German Shepherds as guard dogs that might actually be full-blooded wolves, by the looks of them. They're not tied up. A trespasser is going to get mauled to death one of these days. And Will told me Alex's dad has a shotgun. I've only ever spoken to the mother through the car window. The father never says anything."

"She's very nice," Sandra told her husband. "She invited me in for tea the other day while we were waiting for the boys to return. She served tea from a samovar. We had no difficulty communicating in spite of her thick accent. There were novels on the shelves by Solzhenitsyn and story collections by Anton Chekhov. I recognized those names in Russian. I teach literature," she explained as an aside to Rex. "And also lots of textbooks, though I couldn't make out what they were about."

"Bomb-making?" Rick snorted in derision.

"I thought maybe farming."

"How to grow cannabis?"

"Really, Rick. I never knew you were so prejudiced."

"I'm a realist. We don't know anything about these people, and I do wish you wouldn't encourage Will seeing Alex."

"What makes you think this friend is a militant?" Rex asked in response to Rick Ballantine's earlier comment.

His hand around the glass, Ballantine pointed a finger at Sandra. "My wife found a recruitment website on our son's laptop. Training in Dagestan. 'Kill the infidel and be rewarded with a bevy of virgins in heaven,' sort of thing. Powerful stuff for a teenage boy."

"He said he was doing research for a current affairs essay."

"And you believe everything he says," Ballantine riled at his wife. "Don't Alex's parents come from one of those ex-provinces of imperial Russia where all the dissent foments, either against Russia or the West? Somethingstan?"

"They're from the Republic of Kazakhstan, which used to belong to the Russian Empire and then the USSR, but is now independent," Sandra explained in a mild and neutral tone, as though teaching a class. "And, yes, Islam is the religion of about 70 percent of the population, but let's not jump to conclusions. I'm sure Mr. Graves didn't come to hear about Will's friends or your ... views."

Rex could almost hear the word "narrow" inserted in the slight pause between words and sensed the tension between the couple escalate to a new pitch. An argument was evidently brewing, which would no doubt erupt upon his departure.

He cleared his throat. "Actually, I was interested in a couple who, coincidentally, may be Russian. Early thirties or so. They were looking at homes in the neighbourhood three weeks back. A striking blonde in the company of a well-built, dark-haired fellow. Did you happen to see them around? She was wearing a white fur coat, apparently."

"Fur?" Sandra exclaimed. "In Notting Hamlet? I find that hard to believe!"

"Why do you say that?" Rex asked, remembering Charlotte Spelling's equally surprised reaction to the woman's clothes.

Sandra Ballantine shrugged her slender shoulders. "It just seems out of place. Sort of *nouveau riche*. The residents here aren't like that. We're just ordinary people."

Her husband's tight expression implied that he dissociated himself from the general ordinariness of Notting Hamlet. Rex privately thought the murders had changed that concept. There was, after all, nothing ordinary about four murders all in one day, within less than a one-mile radius.

"I take it then neither of you saw individuals matching that description." Rex sighed in disappointment and set his sherry glass on the table. He made a move to get up from his seat.

Rick Ballantine raised his hand to stop him. "Even if they were genuine buyers, they would have changed their minds after the murders, don't you think? And why are they so important? Who saw these people?"

"Charlotte Spelling, who's selling her house on Fox Lane, and Ernest Blackwell, who told her he'd had a similar-sounding couple, whom he thought might buy his place."

The Ballantines exchanged intrigued glances. "Ernest Blackwell. The first victim found," the husband said. "Well, this couple never made their way here, worst luck. Sounds like they might have had the money to buy."

"Appearances can be deceptive," Rex said, this time retrieving the brolly at his feet and rising from his armchair. "I was hoping to discover whether they had seen anything untoward, since they visited Mr. Blackwell shortly before he was murdered." In a final bid for information, he said, "Lottie Green noticed a new, teal-coloured BMW driving up Fox Lane the day of the murders. I don't suppose either of you noticed anything out of the ordinary?"

Ballantine gazed at the drink in his hand and swirled the melted ice at the bottom of the tumbler. He shook his head in the negative. "Sorry."

"Ah, well." Rex thanked them for their hospitality.

Rick remained seated while his wife, who had likewise shaken her head, saw Rex out the front door. He felt sorry for the bookish woman and hoped he was wrong about his suspicions regarding the strained relations between her and her husband, but even as he reached the foot of the driveway, he heard raised voices behind him.

The rain had stopped and the air felt clear and bracing. A few stars glimmered in the night sky. He stopped suddenly and gazed into space, deep in thought, going back and forth in his mind, weighing possibility versus improbability. Moments later, he resumed his walk at a more brisk pace while drawing the phone from his pocket. His idea seemed like a long shot, but one never knew where an investigation might lead.

TWELVE

By the time Rex returned to Malcolm's house and had removed his coat, his friend was setting the kitchen table and had opened one of the bottles of red wine purchased from the supermarket.

"What's the occasion?" Rex asked, glad not to be eating on his knees in front of the television that evening.

"I decided the food you bought deserved a proper table. There's a film you might like on Channel Four later on. I thought we could have dessert in the sitting room."

"Fine by me. What's the film?"

"A courtroom drama with, uh, I forget his name. But something that might be right up your alley. How did you get on at the Ballantines'? I take it they were in since you were gone awhile." Malcolm folded a pair of blue cotton napkins and placed them on the side plates.

A savoury aroma arose from the oven, and a loaf of crusty French bread stood on the counter ready to be sliced. Rex did the honours.

"I was able to speak to both Sandra and Rick," he replied. "They were quite forthcoming, but couldn't shed any light on the foreign couple. They send their regards, by the way." Rex couldn't remember if they had or not, but it seemed the appropriate thing to say. "Rick Ballantine mentioned he'd worked with you on the project to have an electronic gate put in at the entrance."

"That was a year ago. Never got off the ground. Met with some resistance from the biker crowd."

"So I heard."

"That element didn't exist when Jocelyn and I moved here seven years ago. Ah, well. Shall I take out the cheese?" Malcolm asked, opening the refrigerator. "Dinner will be another twenty minutes."

"Grand. I'm famished."

Malcolm set a wedge of Stilton and a slab of aged cheddar on a cutting board, which he placed on the table along with a tub of margarine.

"No butter?" Rex asked. "And don't start on aboot saturated fats."

"I'm a pathologist, not a dietician. The only time I'm interested in the contents of a person's stomach is to determine approximate time of death by the rate of absorption of those contents and where they might have eaten their last meal."

"Enough said." Rex poured the wine and sat down at table, where Malcolm joined him.

"I didn't know what to do with the box of chocolates you bought, so I put them in the fridge. *Belgian* chocolates," Malcolm emphasized. "Really, you shouldn't have," he said coyly. "Seriously, though. Who are they for?"

"For you, numpkins. To take to a certain lady."

"Who? You don't mean Charlotte?"

"Why not?" Rex tucked into his bread and cheese.

"I think it was you she was interested in. It was the same at uni. Why do women like big, burly redheads?"

"Beats me. But methinks you exaggerate. Anyhow, I thought if you took them over as a thank you, you might insert into the conversation that you're widowed and I'm engaged."

"I don't know," Malcolm said pensively. "I'm out of practice. She might be offended."

"Or flattered. After all, you're single, financially stable, and in pretty good shape. What more could a woman ask for?"

"They ask for a lot, if you ask me. You're lucky to have Helen. Attractive and fun, and with a good head on her shoulders."

"Charlotte strikes me as being the same way," Rex said.

"Look, old chap. You're here to work on a case, not match-make!" And yet Malcolm could not conceal his pleasure at the prospect of doing some courting. "It's hard starting again, isn't it?" he said.

"It is. It's not the crazy-carefree love of our youth. It's a more mature and secure emotion. At least, it is with Helen."

"I'll see how I feel tomorrow," Malcolm allowed.

"You do that."

They ate in companionable silence for a few minutes.

"So what else did you talk about over at the Ballantines'?" his friend asked.

"Their lad, Will, mostly. They have concerns regarding a friend he's spending time with. I gather this Alex's parents are from a part of the former Soviet Union that is home to some Islamist extremists, and Sandra caught her son logged on to what sounds like a terrorist website."

"They're right to be concerned. Look what those two brothers did at the Boston Marathon in the name of Islam."

"Radical Islam," Rex corrected. "Islam is generally a peaceful religion."

"I'm glad I'm not a parent. Who knows what kids get up to these days? You may think they're safe in their room, but the Internet gives them access to all sorts of people you wouldn't want in your home. The parents could put spyware or whatever on Will's computer to monitor what he's doing, but I suppose kids are wise to that. Most of them are more technologically savvy than their parents."

"Fortunately I never had to go through that with Campbell."

"Are you worried about him living in the States?"

Rex munched on a piece of bread before replying. "Not unduly. I never feel under threat when I visit him in Florida."

"Isn't that where the nine-eleven terrorists took flight training? I tell you—nowhere is safe. Not Europe. Not even Notting Hamlet. Oh, I say. Talking about Campbell, am I not his godfather? I fear I've been sorely remiss in his regard."

Rex waved away his concern. "He's a full-grown man now."

"We were very proud that you and Fiona chose us, you know. Jocelyn was the one who remembered the birthday cards and presents at Christmas. I'm hopeless at all the social niceties. I hope Campbell knows I'm here for him if he needs me. He's the closest to a son that I have." Malcolm spoke with feeling. "You know, with Jocelyn gone, I'm all at sixes and sevens." He set down his napkin and stared glumly at his plate of crumbs.

"And likely to remain feeling that way unless you start getting oot more." Rex refrained from telling his friend that part of his reason for making the trip from Edinburgh was because he was worried about him.

"Sometimes I feel this awful, screaming loneliness," Malcolm confided. "It's getting easier, but sometimes I still find it an effort to get out of bed in the morning."

"Here, have some more wine." Rex topped up Malcolm's glass and, to distract him from his gloomy mood, said, "While I was walking back from the Ballantines' house, a thought struck me concerning those three letters. I'd like to hear what you think."

"The letters that resemble my initials? You haven't come to the conclusion that I put them on the victims' foreheads myself, have you?" Malcolm joked.

"Well, of course it occurred to me," Rex said with a smile. "But why would a sane man do such a thing: wipe off the evidence he left, and then confess?"

"I hope the police see it that way. And so your theory is?" The oven timer went off as Malcolm spoke. "Just a sec. Let me concentrate on getting dinner on the table first."

Rex was amused to see his friend wrap a floral apron around his waist and don oven gloves. "Aye, most fetching," he said.

Once the main course was in front of them, Rex resumed. "I wrote those letters down. Somewhere." He searched the pockets of his corduroys. "After what the Ballantines told me regarding Will and his friend, I looked at the letters in a different light." He turned the piece of notepaper to face Malcolm. "What if the middle letter is not a back-to-front *N*?"

"What else could it be?"

"It could be from the Cyrillic alphabet, pronounced *E* in Russian. What if the letters are the word *MIR*?"

"But the letters were M-N-P, same as my initials," Malcolm insisted, looking at Rex in confusion.

Rex tapped his forefinger on the lined paper. "The third letter, which we took to be a *P*, is an *R* in Russian. *MIR* is the phonetic version of the letters you found on the victims."

"As in the space station Mir, you mean?"

"Correct. 'Mir' means world and peace in Russian."

"World and peace? Isn't that an oxymoron? There's conflict breaking out all over the globe, not least in the former Soviet Union."

"Regardless, I don't think that's a dyslexic *N* for Norman," Rex said, underlining it on the paper. "Not when, combined with the other letters, it spells the Russian word for peace and world." If he was right and the police had been apprised of this evidence from the beginning, it would put a different complexion on things. At the very least, it was an alternative explanation for Malcolm's initials.

"Since when do you speak Russian?" Malcolm asked.

"I don't. I remembered seeing the Cyrillic letter we thought was a strange *N* somewhere. I imagine it was hearing about a Russian connection twice in one day that did it." Rex had also discovered on his Google search that upper and lower case were the same in Russian. He felt rather pleased with himself. "This is very good, by the way," he said, pointing his fork at his food.

"Thank you."

"Charlotte mentioned a possibly Slavic accent. And then we have Will's friend who has family from a part of the world where the official language is Russian."

"Should we inform the police?" Malcolm asked, evidently relieved there was another significance to the sinister letters than his own incriminating initials.

"I'd like to pursue this potential clue just a wee bit further first, just to be sure. It may be coincidence the letters spell a Russian word. Much as I dislike coincidences." Rex wondered whether to reveal the extent of his findings to Malcolm at this point. Even after having had a little time to ruminate on the discovery, his theory still seemed fantastic. He was not sure how his friend would react, but Malcolm read his mind.

"There's more, isn't there?" he pressed.

"Aye, maybe. As I was scrolling down the matches for 'MIR,' I discovered that a gang working out of northeast London in the eighties and nineties used that as their gang name. The Russian version."

"How ironic—a peaceful gang!" Malcolm emptied the bottle of Cabernet into their glasses. "Are you seriously suggesting a Russian gang was responsible for our Notting Hamlet murders? Oh, I say, did they bloody their victims in the same way?" he asked with avid interest. "But why would they kill people here?"

"That's what I'd like to know."

"I feel a chill running down my spine," Malcolm said, sitting up in his chair and staring at Rex in shock.

"I admit I felt goose bumps when I came across the gang's name." Such a sensation often meant Rex was onto something. "However, it's a very tenuous lead at this point, so let's keep it under our hats for now."

"The Russkies *here*?" Malcolm exclaimed. "Nobody'd believe that." He shook his head in doubt. "Do you really think so?"

"Or a copycat." Rex sighed and looked at his friend. "So, Malcolm, if you'd left the letters alone, the police might have drawn similar conclusions."

"At least now they know about the letters," Malcolm rebutted sulkily. "What if Walker is connected to the Russian mob?"

"Perhaps he is, and the police are one step ahead of us. I hope the evidence you supplied belatedly isn't thrown oot for being tampered with."

"Okay, I get it, Rex." Malcolm bristled in his chair. "You don't need to keep on about it. What possessed me, I don't know. I just want to make things right."

Rex twiddled the stem of his glass, staring into the remaining wine, which he could not fail to compare to the colour of blood. "Well, the best way to do that is to get at the facts so we can present irrefutable evidence."

"It's time for the film. Do you want to take a break from the case?"

"You go ahead. I'd like to do some more research. Leave all this," Rex told his friend, sweeping his hand over the table. "I'll clear up. I can think things over at the same time."

"Well, if you insist." Malcolm hesitated. "Thank you for everything. You've always been a loyal friend."

"Och, get away with you!" Rex said with an embarrassed laugh. "You've been the same to me."

"Look at us now!" Malcolm joked. "A couple of old duffers at war with the Russian mob!"

A sobering thought if true, Rex thought, with further misgivings at getting involved in the case.

THIRTEEN

THE NEXT MORNING THE sun made a shy appearance, lifting Rex's spirits after a restless night thrashing the case over in his mind. Malcolm had prepared them each a mug of bedtime Horlicks, which they had drunk in the parlour while they reminisced about their college days. Yet the hot malted milk had not helped calm Rex's overactive brain. Normally a deep sleeper, he had been woken by a thud coming from inside the home. Not accustomed to Malcolm's house, he had lain awake for a while in the fussily floral guest bedroom, listening out for further creaks and bumps and wondering what the noise had been, before falling asleep again.

At breakfast he asked Malcolm about it and he replied he hadn't heard anything. Rex told his friend he would stop by Mr. Olson's and offer to take Magic for a walk. The improved weather was sure to bring residents out of their homes this weekend morning after being cooped up for days because of the rain. Malcolm, eager to do some work in the garden, heartily agreed.

"If you're sure you don't need me," he reiterated. "I might run to the garden centre in Godminton. I could make some enquiries into who sold or rented Yvonne Callister her house while I'm at it. I haven't been able to find any other unsolved murders in Bedfordshire matching Chris Walker's M.O. so far. That's if he is our Notting Hamlet killer."

Yvonne Callister was the woman found strangled in her home four years ago, Rex recalled Malcolm telling him. "Aye, you do that. It might be easier if I wander around here on my own. I don't have a fixed plan."

Leaving the house, he saw Win Prendergast in his front garden and waved. They exchanged comments about the weather and Rex said he was going to take Mr. Olson's dog for a walk.

Prendergast rested his pruning shears on the hedge and nodded his head self-importantly. "Now there's an irony. If someone had offed Mr. Olson, it would have been a mercy for the poor old sod. Not in the brutal fashion Ernest and Barry were done away with. I don't mean that. No, with some painless poison. Euthanasia."

"Not sure such a poison exists. At least, not in my experience."

Prendergast's protruding eyes bulged all the more. "Malcolm said you were a Crown prosecutor. I'll bet you've seen all sorts of goings-on."

"Indeed I have." Rex gave the neighbour a friendly nod and set off down the driveway. As he passed Barry Burns's home, he noticed that the For Sale sign had been dug up, leaving a square hole in the lawn. Rex wondered if family would claim the property, and whether Mr. Burns had made a will.

Walking on to Fox Lane, he mentally reviewed the notes he had written up the night before based on his online research and he went over in his mind what steps he could take to confirm or refute his new theory regarding the Russian gang.

Mr. Olson's caregiver, dressed in blue scrubs, flashed his gold teeth at Rex upon opening the front door. Magic barked in short bursts and vigorously wagged his black tail.

"Would you care for some tea before you head out, Mr. Rex?" the young man sang out politely.

"I just had coffee, but thank you. How is Mr. Olson today?"

"Well enough. I'll sit him in the garden later, air him out a bit."

"Best take advantage of the weather while it lasts," Rex agreed, attaching the leash to the dog's collar.

Magic trotted ahead on the path and, once on the sidewalk, availed himself of the first tree. The radio in Malcolm's kitchen had forecast highs in the fifties that day. Already the sun warmed Rex's face and lent a welcoming aspect to the neighbourhood, brightening such greenery as was evident and bathing the timber-fronted façades in mellower hues.

People emerged from their homes as though from hibernation, cautiously peering out of doorways and blinking in the sunlight. The sky, washed of clouds, hung pale blue. An unseen mower started up down the street, while across the road a woman draped a pair of bath mats over a wrought-iron bench to dry.

Rex sauntered back up Fox Lane with the dog, glancing into the front gardens and windows, further acquainting himself with the street where two of the four victims had been murdered. Few signs remained of the event he felt sure the residents would sooner forget. He decided to take Magic up to the top of the "T," where he let him loose to nose along the riverbank behind Malcolm's house. A pungent odour of damp earth and dead leaves permeated the mild autumn air. Rex spotted his friend clipping his yew hedge in his shirtsleeves and then turned his attention to the fields on the other side of the sluggish stretch of river.

The Ivel narrowed to fordable depths at certain points along its course, as he discovered coming upon an angler in waders in one spot and a couple of boys throwing rocks in another, in an attempt to bridge the low banks festooned with reeds. Rex could hear the splash of the stones on the water's surface, swiftly followed by a soft thud as they landed in the riverbed, attesting to the shallowness of the stream.

Beyond the river and flat expanse of fields, a farm shrouded in mist the day before came into sharper focus. The property consisted of a stone cottage and several outhouses, along with an assortment of machinery and what appeared from this distance to be large pails and metal storage tanks. Rex decided to return with Malcolm's binoculars when there were no people about on the river. The pretext of bird-watching might appear weak to any observer, since only crows were visible, circling above the leafless trees.

Further up the murky green ribbon of water, a muddy path cut from the other side directly to the farm. Rex called the dog to heel and, leading him away from the river, traversed the grass square between the two cul-de-sacs. Turning onto Otter Court, he ran into the same lanky teenager from the day before hunched in his charcoal hooded jacket. He was walking from the direction of the Ballantine house, wavy chestnut hair flopping over half his face. Surmising this was Will from Malcolm's confirmation of his description, Rex held his course. However, upon drawing closer, he saw that Will was wearing earphones. Nonetheless, Rex nodded and said hello, and was greeted by a tightly mouthed "hey" or "hi" delivered in a flat monotone. Rex stared after him, repressing a feeling of antipathy for the boy, who continued on his way in his odd, springing gait and suddenly veered onto the green, presumably en route to the Leontiev farm across the river. As far as Rex knew, there was nothing else back there to distract or amuse a boy of Will's age and interests.

Man and dog circled the cul-de-sac and proceeded down Fox Lane, where Lottie accosted them on the street in a spinach green cardigan closed with horn buttons. Grey wisps of hair lifted in the breeze around her weathered face.

"You'll never guess what," she said, stooping to pet Magic. "One of the dogs at forty-seven was poisoned! Its owners took it to the vet last night."

Magic flopped at Rex's feet, panting after his exertions, his tongue lolling out the side of his mouth.

"How do they know it was poisoned?" Rex asked.

"The symptoms. The vet said to look for any household chemicals lying about the home or garage. The owners couldn't find anything and demanded an autopsy. It's a shame, but I can't say I'm all that sorry, because it was a very loud and aggressive dog. Not that big, but with a bark that set my teeth on edge."

"And someone else's teeth, presumably."

"It would attack other dogs. Not like Magic here," Lottie said, fondling his black ears. "You're a nice, quiet doggie!"

"Any suspects?"

"Too soon to say." Thereupon, the elderly woman clammed up her lips as though she knew something but didn't want to speak out of turn.

"I'll tell Mr. Olson, in case that dog wasn't the only target. Unless, of course, it was not deliberate."

"Oh, I'm sure it was. There was a prowler last night," Lottie whispered urgently, glancing about them. "Mrs. Jensen was looking out her bedroom window. This was at about two in the morning and she couldn't sleep. She saw a man loitering between the street lamps, and then he vanished."

"Did she give a description?"

"She thinks he was wearing a black balaclava and perhaps a dark jacket or coat. She said it was too dark to be absolutely sure."

"Not identifiable then," Rex said with a disappointed sigh.

"But definitely a man judging by his size and the way he walked, she told me. Her husband will keep watch tonight. If he turns up again, they're going to call the police."

"Do you have any idea who it might be?" Rex probed.

"I may have my suspicions," Lottie replied with exasperating reticence. "But I don't want to finger-point prematurely."

Either she did know something, Rex surmised, or else she was pretending in order to garner attention. He decided not to press her on the question of the prowler's identity. "Where exactly does Mrs. Jensen live?" he asked instead.

He looked up the street to where Lottie pointed and saw the Jensen home was located almost opposite Charlotte's. Something slipped in his chest. What if the killer had not finished targeting the home sellers of Notting Hamlet? It could be Ms. Spelling was next on the list. And what about the handyman, Randall Gomez, who appeared to have taken an interest in her? The man, by all accounts, had an eye for the ladies. Single ladies. He'd been seeing Valerie Trotter, apparently. Was he stalking Charlotte? Or was someone else?

At that moment, Rex saw a car reversing out of Charlotte's garage. He waved as she drove by and she waved back with a friendly smile. Lottie said goodbye and continued up the street.

If the chemistry teacher, whom Malcolm had told him was always complaining about the dog, had poisoned the animal at number forty-seven, he wouldn't have needed to be out prowling across the street since he lived next door to the murdered pet. Such were Rex's thoughts.

"Nice day," a female voice called behind him.

He spun around to find a woman of late middle years in pink polka dot gardening gloves standing in the garden adjacent to that of the murdered Valerie Trotter. She flexed her back as though she had been bending or crouching in an uncomfortable position. Fading copper curls coiled about an angular face that wrinkled around the eyes and mouth as she smiled.

"A good day for gardening," he agreed.

The woman rested her gloved fists on her hips. "The rain has brought out the weeds."

"It'll do that," Rex said, nodding and smiling back at her.

"Is that Mr. Olson's dog?"

"It is. I've been acting as dog-walker. I'm staying at Malcolm Patterson's in Badger Court for the weekend."

"Oh, bother. There's another one." The woman sunk to her knees and yanked a nettle up by the roots. "I can't abide them," she said, stuffing it into the plastic bag at her feet and straightening up again. "We had another Scottish gentleman in the neighbourhood a month back. John Calpin, I think his name was. I have his card somewhere. A young writer. I don't suppose you know him?"

"I don't think so." Rex drew closer to the fence so he would not have to continue raising his voice to be heard. Magic dragged himself up from the asphalt and plopped down again when Rex stopped.

"Said he was looking for his birth mother and had an inkling she might be living in Notting Hamlet," the woman told him. "He didn't know her name, only that she'd be in her late forties. I felt sorry for the young man and invited him in for a cup of tea. That was before the murders, of course. Now I'd think twice about letting a stranger into my home." She shook her curly head. Rex waited for a "Whatever is the world coming to?" but it never materialized.

"Were you able to help him?" he asked.

"I know a few women who fit that description, but I don't know everybody around here."

"Your neighbour was around that age, wasn't she?"

"It's funny you should say that. I thought of her first. She looked the type to have had a child out of wedlock, if you'll forgive my saying so. She was a bit brassy—not to speak ill of the dead. A nice woman for all that, always pleasant when we ran into each other. Gives me a chill to think what happened to her. Fortunately, it happened in the house up the street and not next door." The woman glanced in the direction of Ernest Blackwell's property. "Killed along with the owner. The other two murders took place on Badger Court, as you've probably heard. Isn't that where you said you were staying?"

"Aye, and it was my friend Malcolm who found them."

"That's right!" The woman shook her head in disbelief. "Just terrible. But I suppose Malcolm Patterson is used to dead bodies.

Better it was him who saw what happened to Ernest Blackwell than Lottie. She only saw part of his body on the floor, not the blood."

"Did my fellow Scotsman ever find his mother?" Rex asked, anxious to return to the previous topic.

"I don't know. I suspect he may have thought it was Valerie Trotter. He was parked across the street opposite her house, staring out his car window as though he might be contemplating buying the property, as I thought at first. Now I realize he may've been waiting for a glimpse of her. But at the time I wondered if he was lost and went over to ask if I could help him."

"Was he driving a bluish green BMW?" Rex asked.

"No, a dark red hatchback that looked like it had a lot of mileage on it. Why do you ask?"

"Someone mentioned seeing an unfamiliar BMW on this street." Rex did not mention it had been spotted on the day of the murders. "Were you able to tell him much about Valerie Trotter?" he asked with kindly interest.

"Only that she'd been living next door for nineteen years—almost as long as I have—and worked as a bookkeeper. He asked about her friends, and I told him I thought she might be seeing another resident, Vic Chandler, though I only saw them together occasionally. If they were an item, they never flaunted it."

Rex did his best to conceal his surprise. Valerie seeing Vic? He thought she was seeing the handyman. "Vic Chandler was another of the victims, wasn't he?" he asked, knowing full well that he was.

The woman nodded knowingly. "And he had his home up for sale as well. All four victims did. I thought Vic and Valerie might be planning to move into a new place together."

"What's happening about her house now? I see the sign's still there."

The woman removed her gloves and shook off the loose earth. "I haven't a clue. Nobody's been round that I know of. But it can't just stay empty, can it? Somebody, if not the bank, will claim it. And yet," she said, frowning in thought, "I seem to remember Valerie saying she paid cash for it."

Magic, patiently dozing in the sunshine until now, uttered a faint whine at Rex's feet and shifted into a sitting position, clearly keen to get off home. Rex patted his sleek black head, thinking of a way to see John Calpin's business card. He could admit he was conducting a private enquiry. After all, it was no real secret and word was bound to get around, but he should have done so upfront. Now it was too late. Finding that people spoke more freely in casual conversation, he hadn't wanted to put the resident on her guard.

"Did you try to contact the young writer after Valerie Trotter's death?" he asked innocuously.

"I thought about it, but finally decided he'd probably see it on the news. What a shock it must have been if he thought Valerie was his mother!"

"Indeed. Ehm, if you like, I could contact him when I get back to Edinburgh. Did he say where in Scotland he hailed from?"

"Glasgow, I think. It's kind of you, but it would probably be better if the call came from me. Yes, I might just do that. He's been rather on my mind since her murder."

"Well, let me give you my card," Rex said. "I'd be interested to hear the rest of the story."

She fished out a pair of reading glasses from the deep pockets of her housecoat. "Rex Graves, QC," she read aloud.

"At your service," he said, holding out his hand.

"Geraldine Prather," she reciprocated.

He bid her goodbye and took Magic home, eager to return to Malcolm's and relay the strange coincidence of a young writer by the name of John Calpin seeking out a woman who had turned up dead a week later.

FOURTEEN

"This takes our investigation in a new direction, doesn't it?" Malcolm said gleefully after Rex had filled him in on his encounter with Geraldine Prather.

The two men sat at the kitchen table over tea and ginger-nut biscuits as the sun peeped through the top half of the window above the red gingham curtain.

"I imagine the police questioned Ms. Prather after Valerie Trotter's murder, since they lived next door to each other," Malcolm continued. "I wonder if she told them about your fellow countryman asking all those questions."

"I should have asked. But I hadn't told her I was actively interested in the case. I don't want too many people knowing."

"It's only a matter of time. Gossip is as rife here as in any other community." Malcolm nibbled on a biscuit. "Are you thinking what I'm thinking?"

"That being?"

"That this man murdered his mother and her lover in a fit of rage over being abandoned at birth?"

"We don't know that she was his mother," Rex pointed out. "Or that she was romantically involved with Vic Chandler."

"Let's say that she was. This Calpin chap kills Ernest Blackwell because he's in the house, and he has to kill Barry Burns because he may have seen something, living across from Chandler."

"Why murder the woman when she was at someone else's house?" Rex objected. "Seems rather risky to me."

"Maybe he thought she was seeing Ernest as well."

"Ernest Blackwell was an old man." Rex dunked his biscuit in his tea. "I'll search the Glaswegian's name online, see if I can come up with any hits. Geraldine Prather said he was a writer. He may have made up the story aboot trying to find his mother to get sympathy and elicit more information."

"You mean, like you made up the story about trying to find your non-existent daughter?"

"*Touché*," Rex conceded. "But strange that this John Calpin should find his mother and she dies so soon after."

"Also strange that an unlikely foreign couple should be looking in Notting Hamlet as well."

"That's at least three suspicious people other than Chris Walker. Did you make any headway with your enquiries concerning Yvonne Callister?" Rex asked, recalling his friend's proposed trip into Godminton.

"That didn't take long. Covington's, the only other estate agent's in Godminton, sold her the bungalow she was strangled in. She paid cash, presumably from her divorce settlement. I told them I was the forensic pathologist in her case and had a personal interest.

Callister was her maiden name, which she retained or reverted to after her divorce. Her ex-husband, I gleaned from old newspaper articles online, was a Paul Cardona."

"She could have looked at properties listed by Chris Walker before deciding on the bungalow."

"True," Malcolm said. "But I asked Lea at his office whether they had an Yvonne Callister on their books from about four years ago. She seemed very suspicious when I enquired, but looked it up and told me no. And she asked if you had found your daughter—in a way that suggested she didn't believe us." He winced as he said this.

"That Lea is no fool." Rex sat back in his chair and let out a vehement sigh. "The police might have mentioned fingerprints belonging to her boss if such had been found in the three Notting Hamlet homes."

"They didn't tell me about his previous police record. Lea divulged that. But Walker was in the victims' houses on business, so it wouldn't be surprising to find his prints on doorknobs and furniture. But his wet shoe print is significant because it puts him at one of the scenes at around the time of the murders."

Rex nodded thoughtfully. "If the police didn't find suspicious fingerprints, the perpetrator must have worn gloves or wiped any prints clean." As was the case with the victims' foreheads, he thought, biting his tongue. "The apparent lack of evidence points to a professional killer or someone familiar enough with police procedure to avoid the obvious pitfalls. And if the killer was Walker, why did he leave a wet shoe print and blood scrawls for the police to find?"

"Search me. He may have missed the wet print when putting his shoes back on. But the letters make no sense if it was him unless he was trying to implicate me or the Russian gang. But that would be dangerous. If word got out, they could come after him if they're still active."

"He's looking less and less like a suspect, as far as I'm concerned." Rex drummed two fingers against the side of his teacup. "His trouble with the law in the past was nothing akin to multiple murders. And I still fail to see what he hoped to gain by killing his own clients."

"Perhaps he snapped," Malcolm said, breaking a ginger-nut in half for emphasis. "He may've decided his ex-wife wasn't going to get any more of his money. What he wrote on the victims might hold special meaning for him. Perhaps the letters stand for her initials or the title of their favourite song. You know, a touch of irony."

Rex regarded his friend with one eyebrow raised. "Perhaps just a wee bit far-fetched?"

"No more so than your Russian space station theory," Malcolm challenged.

"Every theory so far, including that of Chris Walker's guilt, is preposterous, in my view. They all boomerang to the same question: Why would anyone want to kill two old duffers and a middle-aged pair who, by all accounts, kept to themselves? And Chris Walker has other properties. Why restrict himself to offing his Notting Hamlet clients?"

"I'll take that as rhetorical," Malcolm said, reaching for another biscuit in the packet.

"I learnt something else on my walk this morning, aside from what Geraldine Prather told me," Rex said. "Your friend Lottie informed me the barking dog at forty-seven had been taken care of."

"Sounds ominous. Murdered?"

"You look shocked."

"Well, I am. I don't subscribe to murdering animals, however much of a disturbance they might be. And I certainly don't like the sound of another murder around here. Murdered how?"

"Poisoned."

"Lottie didn't tell me any of this!" Malcolm seemed put out.

"Perhaps she phoned while you were in the garden."

"Perhaps," Malcolm relented. "I'll check my messages. What else did she say?"

"Only that the owners took it to the vet and have requested an autopsy."

"It's that character at forty-five, I'll bet; their neighbour who slammed the door in your face."

"Well, they'll need proof he did it."

"He's a chemistry teacher at Will Ballantine's school. Was. Not sure if he's still there. He'd know about poisons."

"Lottie also mentioned that a resident on Fox Lane saw a prowler in the wee hours of this morning loitering on the west side of the street opposite Charlotte Spelling's house."

"Which resident saw this?"

Rex consulted his notes. "A Mrs. Jensen. Is she credible?"

"She's a stalwart churchgoer and runs a thrift shop in Godminton. I eventually took Jocelyn's clothes there. They weren't doing anybody any good hanging in the wardrobe. And I can't abide the smell of mothballs. Mrs. Jensen was very grateful for the donation. Did she get a good look at the prowler?"

"Too dark. And I can't be sure she or Lottie were not elaborating for dramatic effect. In any case, Charlotte looked just fine when she drove by this morning while I was talking to Lottie. Oh, and I ran into Will again on his way to the farm across the river."

"You did have a busy morning." Malcolm lifted the pot of tea. "A refill?"

"Thank you. As I'd hoped, the sun brought oot the good people of Notting Hamlet. Geraldine Prather is a delightful woman. I wasn't able to talk to the lad, though. He was listening to his iPod. He barely made eye contact. I don't think it's just shyness. He seems altogether very introverted."

"I told you he wasn't sociable." Malcolm got up and started clearing the table. "What do you want to do for lunch?"

"We've just had elevenses!"

"I know, but I always have lunch at twelve-thirty."

Rex privately thought his friend was much too set in his ways. He toyed with the idea of bringing up Charlotte again, but was anxious to get on his computer and discover what he could about John Calpin before lunch. "Sandwiches would do me fine," he told his friend.

"Right-oh. Well, I'll go finish up in the garden, unless you need me for anything?"

"You go ahead." Rex set up his laptop, already engrossed in his thoughts.

He hoped Geraldine Prather had remembered the young man's name and place of residence correctly, since that was all he had to go on. How many John Calpins lived in Glasgow, and did any of them exist in cyberspace? Just as well he wasn't John Calvin with a *v*, Rex thought with relief.

He need not have worried. Within minutes, he struck gold. The time flew by in Malcolm's absence. He tapped away on the keyboard and jotted down notes in his lined pad, busying himself in this way without distraction until his host reappeared an hour and a quarter later to make lunch.

"I see you made some headway," his friend remarked, eyeing the filled notepad at Rex's elbow.

"I think I found Ms. Prather's writer." Rex rubbed his hands together in satisfaction. "There are two John Calpins in Glasgow, one a carpenter, the other a journalist. The journalist has a website and had an article published in the *Scotsman* last month. He's the right age to have a mother of forty-seven, as Valerie was, judging by his photo."

He turned his screen around so Malcolm could see the face displayed on the site. The man in question was in his late twenties, wore designer glasses, and sported dark, fashionably spiked hair.

"Looks like a journalist," Malcolm remarked. "Sure he's the right person?"

"Can't be absolutely sure, but something interesting came up in his newspaper article, which could tie in with the Russian connection."

Malcolm spun around from washing his hands at the kitchen sink. "So there really may be something to your Russian theory? You never cease to amaze me."

Rex sat back in his chair and flexed his fingers. "Let me give you the gist of the article first to put things in context. This John Calpin is an up-and-coming investigative reporter and in his piece on British mobsters he draws parallels between the Ice Cream Wars of the eighties in Glasgow and those in Essex."

"Ice Cream Wars?" Malcolm let out a pouf of laughter. "Vanilla versus strawberry?"

"All right, Malcolm. I know it sounds silly, but the feuds between the rival ice cream van operators grew very deadly. Literally. It was really a drug war. The Scottish public eventually got impatient with the police when they failed to control the situation, and began referring to the Serious Crime Squad as the Serious Chimes Squad—after the jingles played on the vans' loudspeakers."

Malcolm burst into full-blown laughter. "You're having me on!" he said, holding his stomach.

Rex shook his head. "I kid you not. Mobsters in the East End of Glasgow ran the operations. The vendors distributed cocaine on their routes, using the ice cream sales as a front." He saw from Malcolm's expression that he had his friend's disbelieving attention.

"You mean they sold illegal narcotics out of their Mr Whippy vans while serving ice cream cones and ice lollies to kids?"

"Exactly so."

"I don't remember seeing that in the news."

"You were probably too busy studying for your medical exams."

"I never seemed to have time for much else." Malcolm gave a regretful sigh. "Alas, my misspent youth."

"Remember those blue-and-white vans?" Rex asked, lost in memories of his own. "You could hear those tinny tunes a mile away. One of my most vivid memories of early childhood is the scent of mass-produced ice cream mingling with the smell of road tar on a hot summer day." He stretched out his arms, which were stiff from being at the computer. "Anyhow, it was a lucrative enterprise and conflicts arose over drug turf. The ice cream scam was adopted by some gangland figures in Essex, namely the Cruikshank Twins. By the nineties, they were selling ecstasy along with the cannabis and Colombian cocaine."

"Did they ever get caught?" Malcolm asked over his shoulder as he prepared sandwiches at the counter.

"No, at least not the twins. Business boomed for Frank and Kevin until a Russian gang spilling over from East London decided they wanted a piece of the action and started arranging nasty accidents for the Cruikshank drivers as they peedled around in their vans with their loudspeakers going at full chime."

Malcolm laughed outright again, and Rex went on more seriously.

"The rival gang, headed by a character aptly named Ivan the Terrible, was downright ruthless. His associates sabotaged the vans, slashing tyres and shooting through the windscreens. They even attempted to kill the Cruikshank family in their home by posting a firebomb through the letterbox. The twins and Kevin's daughter escaped from an upstairs window with only minor burns and smoke inhalation. The arsonists were never charged due to lack of evidence. According to Calpin's article, the Cruikshanks decided it was time to retire. It's widely believed they forged new identities and moved to Australia."

"That's where we sent our convicts in the good old days. Nice of them to save us the trouble. But what does this have to do with our case?"

"While the Cruikshanks were in business, Kevin's daughter Sylvia kept the books. A fourth member of the gang, Fred Forspaniak, aka Fred the Spanner, was their main enforcer. He served two years inside for GBH."

"That's a light sentence for grievous bodily harm at the mob level. Oh, I get it now." Malcolm brought two side plates to the table. "You're saying the twins, daughter, and this Fred chap didn't go to Australia after all, but hid out in Notting Hamlet. Well, they're Down Under now," he said with jocularity.

"Aye, it seems the past caught up with them. There's a nephew too," Rex continued, "but he's still in HMP Belmarsh for extortion and money laundering. That's a photo of him." He pointed to the article onscreen. "There's none depicting the rest of the gang, unfortunately. But why would they turn up dead after all this time?"

"I'm sure you'll find out," Malcolm said, grinning with just a hint of condescension. "Doesn't look like much, does he?" he jeered at the nondescript nephew in the photo.

Rex thought his friend in an uncharacteristically good mood, but was too absorbed in the matter at hand to pay it much mind. "The four victims moved here almost twenty years ago. Ernest and Barry were Essex boys. And Valerie, who could be Sylvia, was a bookkeeper. I've definitely got the goose bumps, Malcolm."

"It's all beginning to make more sense," his friend agreed as he deposited a platter of sandwiches between them with a grandiose flourish. "Curried egg salad." He paused for a moment as he contemplated his creation.

"Malcolm, whatever is wrong with you? You look all mooney."

"If you must know, I saw Charlotte just before lunch and gave her the chocolates."

"Well, well. You sly old dog. And?"

"I caught her as she was returning from the post office. She was quite receptive to my overtures, I think. I managed to sneak in the fact that you're engaged and I've been a widower for three years. She was very sympathetic. It appears she lost someone special too. In a car accident."

"I applaud you, Malcolm. Such a bold step deserves a beer." Rex got to his feet to retrieve two cans from the refrigerator.

"And you deserve praise for your work on the case. I knew I could count on you!"

"Not so fast," Rex said. "It's all supposition at this point."

Malcolm suddenly appeared solemn. "But if the Russkies *are* responsible for the murders and find out about our involvement, our goose is cooked. Look what they did to my neighbours."

"Most uplifting, Malcolm." Rex shot his old college friend a look loaded with sarcasm.

"Don't mention it."

Were the Russian mafia really involved? A chill slid down Rex's spine. This was a potentially dangerous situation, beyond anything he had encountered before, and he suddenly felt out of his depth.

FIFTEEN

REX CONTINUED HIS RESEARCH after lunch while Malcolm was in the garden finishing the work he had abandoned to see Charlotte. He could hear his friend digging somewhere out back by the river, the shovel scraping into the gritty earth. Pausing in his online reading, Rex wondered if they should warn Charlotte about Mrs. Jensen's prowler and the poisoning of the dog, in case she had a dog. Charlotte Spelling was alone in her house and the fact it was for sale could not be ignored.

He got up from his chair and looked under "Spelling" in the directory by the phone in the hall. Not bothering to put on a coat, he exited the kitchen door to the back garden, where he found Malcolm, spade in hand, uprooting a tangle of brambles.

"It's warmed up nicely," Rex commented, looking towards the river where beams of light played off the water visible a short distance away between the reeds and bushes, turning the surface from cold pewter to sea glass green.

Malcolm leaned his forearm against the wooden handle of his gardening implement. "Glorious weather," he agreed. A sheen of perspiration coated his face, which had lost some of its usual pallor as a result of being out in the wind and sun. A renewed energy in his movements added to the impression of newfound vigour. Rex was in no doubt as to its cause.

"Have you come to help?" his friend asked. He pointed to Rex's feet. "You'll need sturdier shoes."

"Actually, I came to ask if you had Charlotte's number. She's not listed in the phone book."

"I don't. I thought it too forward to ask for it earlier. Why?"

"I thought maybe we should tell her aboot the man lurking across the street from her house last night, if you haven't already."

"It would only frighten her. I think we already did a good job of that yesterday. If Lottie was really concerned, she would have called me about it, but there were no messages."

"All the same, I feel it would be remiss not to warn Charlotte, especially if, heaven forbid, something were to happen. I got the impression speaking with her yesterday that she doesn't have much to do with the neighbours, so I doubt she's heard."

Malcolm wiped the sweat from his brow with his shirt sleeve. "Right, well, leave it to me," he said. "It'll give me another excuse to go and see her."

"Do you need more chocolates?" Rex joked.

"Very funny." Malcolm grinned boyishly and went back to his digging. Just then, the phone trilled from the house. "That might be Lottie now," he said, one foot poised on the base of the shovel. "To tell me about the dog poisoning. Or it might be a nuisance telemarketer."

"I'll get it," Rex offered, heading back. "I'll call you if it's urgent."

He trotted to the back door, wiped his feet on the mat, and hurried to the ringing phone. "Hullo, Rex Graves speaking," he announced upon picking up the handset.

"Oh, Rex," a female voice replied at the other end of the line. "This is Charlotte. I was expecting Malcolm."

"Sorry to disappoint," he said in good humour.

"Not at all. Is he available? I wanted to thank him for the delectable chocolates."

"He's in the garden attacking a bramble patch. I'll go fetch him."

"Not if he's busy. But if you could give him my mobile number. It's the only way to reach me as I'm not in the book."

"Be glad to." Rex wrote down the digits, thinking Malcolm would be glad she had called. And it was a lucky coincidence she had. "While I have you on the phone," he said, "I wanted to advise you of something I heard from Lottie this morning. In case nobody mentioned it to you."

"No. What?"

"A prowler was spotted by Mrs. Jensen, who lives across the street from you. At around two this morning."

"Doing what, exactly?" Charlotte asked sharply, and Rex wished he hadn't had to be the one to deliver the sinister news.

"She saw a man keeping to the shadow zones between the street lamps, possibly wearing a balaclava."

Charlotte laughed unexpectedly. "Sorry, but isn't that just too ludicrous to be believed? I mean, really." She giggled again. "And all because the lady loves Milk Tray?"

"Come again?"

"Remember those adverts where a man in a balaclava rappels down the side of a building and enters a window, and then presents a box of chocolates to a woman in a negligée? That's what your description reminded me of. I suppose it's because I have chocolates on my mind."

"Oh, I see." Rex smiled. "Do they still run that ad?"

"I don't know. I don't watch much telly."

"Well, I just wanted to pass that information on. Better safe than sorry, if you'll pardon the cliché. Make sure you lock up at night. In fact, all the time for now." The four murders had been conducted in broad daylight, after all.

"I will, and I appreciate your concern, Rex. Bye now," Charlotte breathed into the phone, and she hung up before he could respond or ask if she had a dog.

A sense of guilt niggled at him as he stood with the phone in his hand and tried to fathom why. Guilt for enjoying the caressing sound of her voice? For speaking and joking with her when Malcolm should have been having that conversation? Guilt for worrying her with some silly gossip? Irritated without quite knowing the reason, he replaced the receiver and went to tell Malcolm that Charlotte had called and left her number.

"I warned her aboot the prowler, but she didn't seem unduly concerned," he reported. He didn't mention the anecdote about the Cadbury chocolates. At least he hadn't called her Charlie, the nickname she went by—as she'd mentioned the day before.

"Do you think I should ask her out for dinner?" Malcolm looked eager, evidently pleased she had taken the initiative to call. "Strike while the iron's hot, sort of thing? But it's Saturday. What if she already has a date?" Frowning, he kicked the shovel loose of clods of earth.

"Then you'll find oot one way or the other. But she did phone to thank you for the chocolates and to leave her number," Rex encouraged his friend.

"Right," Malcolm said, perking up. "And she must have gone to the trouble of looking mine up since I never gave it to her."

Rex experienced a bizarre feeling of déjà vu, of being back at university trying to gauge a girl's interest and debating whether or not to ask her out. Malcolm had always been a vacillator in that regard.

"The King's Head or perhaps something fancier? There's a nice Italian restaurant on the high street in Godminton."

"Ask her," Rex suggested.

"Oh, I say, you don't mind me leaving you at home, do you? Why don't you come along? It might be less awkward."

"Not for me. I'd feel like a third wheel. And I can easily fend for myself."

"Anyway, it may be moot, since she may have other plans." Malcolm took the spade to the shed, relatched the door, and returned without his gardening gloves. They walked back to the house.

"'Once more unto the breach, dear friends, once more,'" Malcolm quoted from Shakespeare's *Henry V*. "What if she says no?"

Rex pushed his friend towards the hall phone where he had left Charlotte's number and retreated to the kitchen, closing the door behind him. All but oblivious to the murmur of Malcolm's voice down the hall, he focused on his research where he had left off half an hour previously.

———

John Calpin's article in the *Scotsman* hinted at revelations in his upcoming book, *Baddest British Mobsters*, due out in August of the following year from Penworth Press. The exposé had simply summarized the Glasgow Ice Cream Wars of the eighties and showed how the Cruikshank Twins had successfully implemented the model in Essex, thereby attracting the attention of a Russian gang operating out of northeast London. Rex felt he might be getting closer to solving the riddle of the Russian letters, even though the article made no mention of them. It was elsewhere that he had read about a London gang using *МИР* as their symbol. What if it were the same gang, he thought with excitement.

The article was merely a teaser. More was to be divulged in the journalist's book. Rex wished he could get his hands on it now.

Malcolm burst into the kitchen. "She said yes! We're going to the King's Head. I'd better go up and shower. Shirt and tie, or pullover?"

"Pullover."

"And you're sure you don't mind?"

"Of course not. I'm up to my eyes in research. You know how I get." A few hours of peace from Malcolm would be a boon, Rex thought, and he was happy that Charlotte had accepted his dinner invitation. His friend definitely needed more of a social life.

Malcolm left the room in a whirl and Rex heard him run up the carpeted stairs. Minutes later, the sound of water gushing through the pipes signified his friend was in the shower. The drowned-out words of a tuneless song reached him from the bathroom as he considered the implication of the words on his screen and how they might relate to the Notting Hamlet murders.

Frank Cruikshank, he learned, was most often referred to as Frankie in references to the notorious Essex gang. Rex remembered the name Frankie coming up in a conversation with a resident and reviewed his notes. He quickly found what he was looking for. Ernest had mentioned the name to Lottie in the context of it being time for him and Frankie to move on. A slip-up, no doubt, on Ernest's part. The name was such a coincidence that Rex all but concluded Ernest and Barry were the elusive gangland twins, and if Frankie had been Barry in his new identity, Ernest had been Kevin, or Kev, as he'd been commonly known. He had also gone by "Kevlar Kev" or just Kevlar.

Online sources alluded to Kev as the leader of the gang, a man not to be trifled with and who had managed to avoid justice at every turn, thus earning him the sobriquet. Perhaps the fact he had escaped the arson attack on his family and other mob hits had reinforced his reputation for invincibility.

Rex unearthed a second photo of the nephew who had overseen the ice cream vendors and controlled their runs. Darrell Cruikshank had also directed the family's bookmaking, loansharking, and other nefarious activities until an investigation by MI5 and the Inland Revenue resulted in his imprisonment. Darrell had not given up his uncles, which had presumably done nothing to commute the length of his sentence, and he was only due for release in October of this year, according to the online information. "Wait a minute," Rex said aloud. "That's last month!" He would make enquiries first thing Monday morning at the high-security prison where Darrell had resided for twenty years at Her Majesty's pleasure.

Malcolm popped his head round the door, his face scrubbed pink and his hair, neatly parted at the side, still damp from his shower. "Wish me luck."

"The best."

"How's the research coming along?" Dressed in dark slacks and a navy blue crew-neck sweater, Malcolm approached the table where Rex was working.

Rex gave his friend a brief overview of his findings, including an account of the Cruikshank family's "financial services" in ironic quotation marks.

"So the Cruikshanks were not only drug traffickers, but loan sharks?" Malcolm whistled softly.

"Correct. Not nice people."

"Do we really care that they're dead?" his friend asked. "That's if they are, in fact, our Notting Hamlet victims."

"That's not the point. Somebody murdered them and we undertook to discover who. The nephew was supposed to have been released from Belmarsh in October." Rex scratched his beard. "He may well have an axe to grind with his family's murderer and want to see them brought to justice. I wonder if he would talk to me. Anyway, get off with you. You don't want to be late on your first date with Charlotte."

"Heavens, no. See you later. Don't work too hard." Malcolm accompanied his admonishment with a smile, knowing from experience that Rex would do just that. "And don't forget to eat."

"Stop fussing!" Rex shooed him off in jovial spirits, and Malcolm left.

The garage door clanged open and shut and the sound of Malcolm's car grew fainter. Through the kitchen window Rex saw it was already growing dark. Easing back into his project with full concentration, he managed to find old photographs of the Cruikshank twins and, though in grainy black-and-white, they showed they were not identical. In their new lives in Notting Hamlet, Ernest and

Barry were 81 and 79 years old respectively, no doubt to disguise their true identities better.

Rex also found a photo of the daughter, Sylvia, leaving the Old Bailey in 1995 after her father was acquitted of a murder, but she bore little resemblance to the picture of Valerie Trotter from the media photo, procured Rex knew not where. One police mug shot showed Fred the Spanner as a young man, before his disfiguring scar, though he had never been an Adonis. Compared to the recent newspaper photo, there could be no doubt he was Vic Chandler: the same bullet-shaped head, pug nose, and prominent ears, though he had taken to shaving off his hair, or what remained of it.

The background material on the Cruikshank gang suggested organized crime had not been a family business before the twins saw the potential of selling drugs in the as-yet unsaturated market of Essex, a county endowed with ports and strategic proximity to London. Born to an Irish Catholic gas meter reader and his wife Eileen, Kev and Frankie Cruikshank grew up in Clacton-on-Sea, the eldest of nine children, but hadn't recruited among their brothers and sisters. In fact, they seemed to have made it their mission to improve the lives of their siblings by footing the bills for vocational training, as well as extracurricular school activities for the youngest of them. The screen began to blur. Rex rubbed the inner corners of his eyes between thumb and forefinger. Tired from staring at the computer, he went back to his notes and read over his interviews with the residents.

Ernest Blackwell and Barry Burns had portrayed themselves as amiable old duffers, no doubt playing up their senile ailments, and had acted the part of good neighbours without, however, getting too close to the other residents. Ernest's dread of hospitals made abundant sense now in light of his new identity. Lie low and avoid all risk of detection would have been his mantra, as with the rest of the gang.

The twins had golfed together, no one suspecting their blood relationship. Valerie, the erstwhile Sylvia, had visited Ernest for lunch that fateful day, a natural thing for a daughter to do, and had maintained ties, romantic or purely friendly, with the fictional Vic Chandler, whose photo clearly denounced him as Fred, the main intimidator and enforcer for the Cruikshank Twins.

Rex had to hand it to them. The four members of the Essex gang had pulled off quite a coup maintaining their anonymity for two decades in a small community where everybody made it a point of knowing everybody else's business.

While continuing to scour the Internet for further information, his cell phone bleeped. A text message from Helen reported she and Julie had boarded the flagship they were cruising on from Miami to the Southern Caribbean. Accompanying photos of their ocean-view cabin boasted a picture window and two bathrooms. More luxurious and spacious than Malcolm's guest bedroom, Rex noted. He responded, and they continued to exchange messages until the bulb in the Tiffany light above the kitchen table went out, leaving only the under-cabinet strip lighting as illumination. Not a problem for reading his phone or computer screen, but a strain on his eyes for his notes, written in his small, precise hand.

When Helen signed off, he got up to look for a replacement bulb, checking first under the sink among the various detergents and sponges, and then in the laundry room. After searching without luck, he thought about calling Malcolm, but ultimately decided not to interrupt his date for something so trivial. The next most likely place he could think of was under the stairs so he made for the hall.

The cupboard lit up with the pull of a string and revealed a narrow, cobwebby space in which he was forced to bow his head. As he was rummaging among the shelves for the spare light bulbs, a dark woollen garment fell to the floor. Picking it up, he was so shocked to see what it was that he inadvertently banged his head on the low ceiling and swore, both from pain and the disturbing surprise of what he had found. He held in his hand a black balaclava.

SIXTEEN

Rex placed the balaclava on the kitchen table, anxious to ask Malcolm about it as soon as he returned from the pub. Unable to concentrate fully on his research, he heated up a carton of soup and cut two thick slices of bread. It seemed pointless to spend more time exploring a gang angle to the murders if Malcolm knew more than he let on. Rex could not begin to comprehend what his friend was doing skulking about the neighbourhood at night wearing a ski mask.

He clung to the hope that his friend had not worn it. And yet, it had been at the top of the pile of scarves and gloves in the stair cupboard, and Rex was almost certain he had heard a noise in the house late the previous night, something falling, perhaps, or a door slamming shut. The exterior kitchen door stuck a bit and required a shove to open and close properly. And the kitchen was directly beneath his guest bedroom. "Oh, Malcolm, what is going on?" he asked himself.

He had not mentioned the balaclava to his friend, since Mrs. Jensen had not been absolutely certain about the person's clothes. If he had divulged this detail, would Malcolm have hidden the bonnet? That would have been a sure indication of guilt. How would he react when he saw it on the table? Rex recalled too that his friend hadn't wanted to tell Charlotte about the prowler at first. Some of Malcolm's behaviour had been dodgy, not least his wiping away of potentially crucial evidence. How involved was Malcolm, in reality, in the Notting Hamlet murders? Rex grew increasingly uneasy.

He poured himself a glass of wine, resolved to reserve judgement until his friend got home. Hopefully, Malcolm could supply a believable explanation for his nocturnal escapade, or else be able to convince him he had not worn the headgear at all.

Mercifully, he did not have long to wait. As he was clearing away the dishes from his light supper, he heard a car engine in the driveway and the garage door open with a jarring clang. He prepared himself. When Malcolm walked in from the laundry room leading from the garage, Rex was drying his wine glass and summoning all his composure.

"All right?" Malcolm asked, smiling. Rex noticed he was wearing a dark jacket and grasping a rolled-up newspaper, which he held up, failing to notice the balaclava on the kitchen table. "You'll never guess what."

"I didn't expect you back so soon," Rex said. "How did it go with Charlotte?"

"Quite well, I think. We have quite a lot in common, actually. She likes sci-fi and Thai food. Didn't ask me in for a nightcap, though. I think I'll have a glass of that Beaujolais." Malcolm deposited the newspaper on the counter while he opened an upper cabinet and reached for a wine glass.

"What's in the paper?" Rex enquired, still troubled by the balaclava, but curious as to why Malcolm would have the *Sun* newspaper on him. He knew about his friend's aversion to the tabloids, so for him to pick one up and bring it home meant it must contain something momentous.

"It was left on our table at the pub. I wouldn't ordinarily have glanced at the *Sun*, but something caught my eye."

"Well?" Rex asked while Malcolm silently poured them both a glass of wine, filling the one Rex had dried and left on the workspace.

"Your journalist John Calpin has been murdered, that's what."

Rex grabbed the newspaper. It took only a minute to read the story, which was graphic in content and sensationalistic in style. "Dear God," he said, looking at Malcolm.

"Didn't you watch the news?" his friend asked.

"I haven't left the kitchen all evening. This is most disturbing." Rex slapped the paper back down on the counter. "The vicious nature of Calpin's murder bears the hallmark of the ones committed here."

"Only worse," Malcolm said. "The murders are all personal in nature, aren't they? I'd go so far as to say revenge killings. I wonder if Calpin's murder had anything to do with his snooping around Notting Hamlet asking after his birth mother."

"I'd say it has everything to do with it, but I don't think he was really trying to find his birth mother. That might have been a ruse. I think he was on to something. Something big. I think in the course of his research on the Cruikshank gang, he discovered they might be living in Bedfordshire. He was doing research for his book on British mobsters, remember, and the question of where the gang disappeared has always been something of a mystery. Presumably, not everyone bought the story of their absconding to Australia."

Malcolm concurred with a grave nod. "Someone found out what John Calpin was up to and abducted him. According to the *Sun*, he was first reported missing in Glasgow three weeks ago, but a grown man going missing doesn't usually make headline news."

"Especially reporters, who are prone to taking off at a moment's notice to follow a story," Rex added. "It's only now his body's been found so horrifically mutilated that we're hearing aboot it. I think he unwittingly led his assassin here and the killer lost no time making sure the four victims couldn't leave Notting Hamlet and disappear again." He took a much-needed gulp of wine. The body count was mounting.

"Calpin may've been tortured to give up their whereabouts before he could publish his findings. It almost put me off my dinner when I read about it," Malcolm said with a pained expression. "And you know I'm not normally squeamish. The article doesn't say if he was dead before he had his eyes plucked out of their sockets, and all the rest of it."

"It says he was shot execution style, so hopefully he talked and died before they went to work on him. The removal of his eyeballs and other body parts may have been symbolic."

"A statement." Malcolm nodded, gazing into his glass of red wine. "A sort of variation on 'See no evil, hear no evil, speak no evil.' And write no evil."

"Aye, they would have been sending a clear message. A journalist needs his ears, eyes, tongue, and hands to report. The extensive mutilation can't have been simply to prevent identification, since there's no mention of his teeth going missing as well."

"If he hadn't been dredged up from the river, no one would have known what happened to him. Mind you, the water wasn't very deep. The Glasgow police are saying they think it was a professional hit. I caught that on TV at the pub." Malcolm wandered towards the table and stopped short when he saw the balaclava. "I could've sworn I put that under the stairs."

"You did. I retrieved it."

Malcolm looked at him in confusion, his face colouring. "Why?"

"Mrs. Jensen thinks her prowler may have been wearing a balaclava," Rex explained, striving to keep his tone neutral. "I needed to replace the bulb in this lamp and, not wanting to disturb you at the pub, I searched high and low and finally found a spare, along with this ski mask." He set down his glass on the counter and calmly folded his arms while he waited for Malcolm to explain.

His friend expelled a long breath. "Well, you caught me out. Nothing gets past you, does it, Rex?" he said with reproach.

"I just cannot credit it," Rex burst out, succumbing to his pent up emotion. "First, tampering with evidence, and now this! What were you doing? Are you trying to get yourself arrested?"

"I couldn't sleep. I was worried about Charlie. I kept seeing that pervert, Randall Gomez, when I closed my eyes. I convinced myself she was in danger, either from him or from some other person hell-bent on killing any resident selling their home. I decided to go out and do a recce of the neighbourhood, and see who else might be out and about at that hour. I needed to reassure myself Charlie was safe and no one was trying to break in."

"Here I am working diligently on your behalf, and you're out at some ungodly hour playing silly beggars!"

"I know, but I feel so useless. I need to be doing something!" Malcolm clenched his fists in impotent rage. "The police still patrol the community, but less and less frequently."

"We are doing something, Malcolm. But if you're so concerned aboot preventing crime in the community, start up a neighbourhood watch, why don't you? Don't go around lurking in the shadows in a black balaclava!"

Charlotte's joke about the masked action man delivering chocolates was not so wide off the mark after all, Rex thought wryly, even though Malcolm made for an unlikely Milk Tray candidate. "Why did you wear this?" He lifted the ski mask and let it fall back on the table.

"It was ruddy cold last night, and I didn't want to take my car in case it was recognized."

Rex sighed in despair. "You're your own worst enemy, Malcolm. Don't go wandering around at night again. Please."

He wondered if he should get hold of Mrs. Jensen and tell her she and her husband didn't need to keep watch tonight. It was not yet nine; not too late to call. However, that would involve revealing the identity of the nitwit in the ski mask and perhaps it would not be such a bad thing to maintain a vigilant eye on the street.

"I won't wear it again at night," his friend promised. "Charlie assured me her alarm system is guaranteed to keep intruders at bay. A distress signal connects directly to the switchboard at Godminton Police Station."

"It could take the police fifteen minutes to get here in the best of conditions." Rex was tired of explaining the obvious. Enough had been said that night about the case. "Why don't you tell me aboot your evening with the lovely Charlotte," he said, still exercised with Malcolm, but ready to change topic. "You didn't discuss the article with her, did you?" he asked, suddenly anxious that Malcolm might have been loose-lipped after a few drinks at the pub.

"When she saw my reaction, she wanted to read it. She was horrified, but didn't understand the significance. She just saw it as another murder, although more brutal than most. And the fact the victim was so young and clean-cut made it worse." Malcolm glanced at the paper, which showed a photo of the victim. "All I said was the story might have some bearing on our case. That's all. I didn't get into the specifics and I thought it better not to call you about it in her company, which, in any case would have come off as rude. Actually, she seemed more interested in asking about you. What your interest in the Notting Hamlet carnage was, and so on. I told her you were gaining a reputation for solving murder cases."

"Oh, Malcolm, you didn't." Rex gazed ruefully at his glass. "It's not a good idea to draw attention to ourselves," he chided his friend. "Especially after this." He pointed to the newspaper, which clearly indicated that, if John Calpin's death was connected to the Notting Hamlet murders, the killer or killers were still at large and not slowing down. "It would be interesting to know if our house agent visited Glasgow," he added. "But somehow I doubt it."

Chris Walker was looking more and more like an innocent man. And the killer more and more like a monster.

SEVENTEEN

THE NEXT DAY ON a sunny and blustery morning, Rex set out to Geraldine Prather's house on Fox Lane carrying the newspaper Malcolm had brought back from the pub. He had gone back and forth in his mind about whether to show her the article and finally decided he should, since it had been she who had told him about John Calpin in the first place. But for her, he would never have known about this latest victim's connection to Notting Hamlet.

There was only one way to find out what Calpin had known, Rex decided, and that was to contact his editor at Penworth Press. Something in the unpublished book might reveal information about the Cruikshank gang or the rival Russian operation that merited five murders and point him in the right direction. For the present, he felt he had to console Geraldine Prather, who had taken a sympathetic interest in the young man.

He had stepped onto the road to cross over to her house when a bicycle swerved in front of him and skidded to a stop. It was a lime green Peugeot racing bike with drop handlebars, the front basket piled with folded newspapers. The rider, a boy of about fourteen with a ferrety face and tawny hair tousled by the stiff breeze, asked, "You a rozzer?"

A stuffed canvas bag slung across his thin chest revealed more Sunday papers.

"Do I look like a policeman?" Rex had to admit he could pass for an inspector in his walking shoes and heavy overcoat, his trimmed reddish beard lending an air of maturity, his pale complexion suggesting a job that mostly confined him to an office.

"People are saying you been asking questions 'bout the murders." The lad's voice, not fully broken, was alternately hoarse and fluty.

"I'm an advocate in Scotland. That's a barrister here. You have something to tell me?"

"Depends, dun'it?"

Rex took the hint. "A bit of extra money to supplement your round—if you have valuable information."

The boy wiped his nose on the back of his hand and looked around the street. It was still early and the residents were presumably taking advantage of a Sunday lie-in and a late breakfast.

"What's your name, lad?"

"Never you mind."

"Didn't your mum ever tell you to watch your manners?" Rex asked evenly, for it took more to rile him than a snivelling brat.

"I don't have no mum, do I? I live with my uncle Bill."

"Would that be Big Bill, leader of the local motorcycle club?"

"How'd you know?" the boy asked, eyes narrowing.

"Like you said, I've been asking a lot of questions. Did the police question you?"

"No. I don't like rozzers. None of my family does."

Probably because they lived on the wrong side of the law, Rex reasoned. If they sold weed, they might well indulge in other illicit activities they didn't want the police knowing about.

He took a deep and patient breath. "You seem like a sharp lad. Did you see anything of interest the day of the murders? But it was a Thursday, so you were probably at school."

"Wasn't. I was riding up here on my bike."

Rex refrained from asking why he had been playing truant. The important thing was that the boy might have seen something. "And?" he prompted. He pulled a crisp £10 note from his wallet.

"Two tenners, mister."

"This for starters. We'll see what your information is worth."

The boy took the money and zipped it into his jacket pocket.

"Oi, where's my paper?" an unshaven man in a blue-striped dressing gown bellowed from his doorstep.

The boy wheeled his bike around Rex, plucked a newspaper from his basket, and winged it towards the house where it landed with a slap on the path. He had a good arm for such a skinny lad, Rex noted. Clasping the front panels of his dressing gown together in one hand, the man bent down and retrieved the paper, and went back inside his house.

Just as Rex was wondering if the boy was going to renege on their deal and take off with his cash, he circled back around and planted his scuffed trainers on the ground, on either side of the pedals.

"There was this shiny new Beamer, yeh? A cross between blue and green, just gorgeous. It was driving slowly up the street. Next thing I knew, the back window rolled down and an old geezer gave me this look. Right freaky. His eyes were hidden by shades, and it wasn't even sunny that day. I was thinking I should get home before it rained, as I was off school with a cold."

"What else can you tell me about this man?" Rex asked with mounting interest.

"He was wearing a fur hat with flaps over his ears and was smoking one of them fat cigars. I got out of there quick and headed home. They would've had to do a U-y to chase me, and I'm dead fast on my bike." The boy sounded breathless by the end of his account, his eyes stretched open from the relived fear of his encounter.

"How old was the man, exactly?"

"He was a fossil. He had wrinkly cheeks and red streaks on his nose. Oh, yeh, and he was wearing leather gloves and a thick coat."

"Who else was in the BMW?"

"Just him in the back. The windows were tinted and I couldn't see who was driving, but there was somebody sitting in the passenger seat."

"And that's all you saw?" Rex asked. A car passed behind him, but he didn't look 'round, focused as he was on the teen, who was beginning to fidget as his gaze drifted down the street where he had yet to deliver his papers. "What time was this?"

"Late morning, wan'it?"

Rex produced a twenty from his wallet and held it out to the boy. His story corroborated Lottie Green's and provided a description of one of the occupants of the vehicle. There was no reason to doubt the additional details.

The boy's eyes widened at the sight of the extra money.

"Here's my card, in case you remember anything else."

"My name's Danny."

"Take care, Danny." Rex strode on to Geraldine Prather's house with a light step and a lighter wallet.

When she opened the front door he saw she was teary-eyed and clasping a tissue. She wore a green crêpe de Chine blouse over slacks, and pale pink ballet shoes, a chic transformation from her gardening clothes of the day before. Her fading copper coils were pinned back from her temples, her lipstick and powder in place, yet her expression was distraught.

"I've caught you at a bad time," Rex apologized.

"I was on my way to church when I saw the story about John Calpin." She indicated the rolled newspaper in Rex's hand. "Is that what you came to tell me?"

"I was not sure if you'd heard. My friend picked this up at the pub last night."

"Come in," she said briskly in an obvious effort to pull herself together. "I put some coffee on." She led him into the living room, where the walls and soft furnishings were decorated in deep jewel tones, with a few choice antiques interspersed among the sofas and chairs. The house plan was the same as Charlotte's, but it projected a more formal feel. White plantation blinds filtered light from the windows and broke up the view of the front garden and street into narrow horizontal strips.

Rex made himself comfortable in one of the embroidered wing armchairs while Geraldine Prather left the room to prepare the coffee. He reread the article in the *Sun* and hoped the version in her paper was less lurid. She returned with a porcelain coffee pot and matching crockery on a tray, which she deposited on a lacquer table beside him.

"I lost my husband to a stroke." She filled two cups and invited Rex to help himself to cream and sugar. "It must be worse when you lose someone to a violent death. Dreadful that John was only identifiable through his dental records." Her hand trembled as she lifted the jug of cream. "The paper said he was the son of Robert and Elspeth Calpin, but didn't mention if he was adopted. But it probably wouldn't, would it? The parents must be heartbroken."

"I have a son in his twenties. It's never easy to lose a child, but when they're just starting out in life and beginning to fulfil their potential, it must be especially hard. I made enquiries. John Calpin was evidently very talented. He had a book in the works."

"A novel?" Geraldine asked with keen interest.

"Non-fiction. An investigative piece on notorious British mobsters. True crime, I think they call it."

"Will it still be published?"

"Might depend on how far along he was with it."

"I wonder if his adoptive parents know he was searching for his birth mother. Seems such a tragic coincidence they should both end up murdered—if it was my neighbour, Valerie."

"Perhaps not a coincidence," Rex remarked, without, however, wishing to reveal too much.

"Whatever do you mean?" Geraldine asked.

"Do we know for a fact he was trying to find his birth mother? It might have been a cover for something else he was investigating in Notting Hamlet."

"Oh, I see." Mrs. Prather looked disappointed that the young man might have lied to her. "I never connected the dots," she said. "What with him being murdered up in Glasgow."

"Well, it's just conjecture on my part," Rex hastened to add. "As a prosecutor, I tend not to accept coincidence at face value."

"There was no reference in my paper to the murders here. Was there in yours?"

"None. I'm assuming the police are not aware John Calpin was in Notting Hamlet."

"Should I contact them?"

"I would. I'm looking into the matter myself, and I will be contacting the police regarding a few other matters that have come to light. Malcolm asked me to look into the case. It was an opportunity to spend some time with him and see how he was faring. He took his wife's death very hard."

"I knew he was a widower. So very sad. How did she die? I forget."

"A fall down the stairs. She suffered from migraines. She was having a bad spell and lost her balance." Rex remembered Jocelyn as rail thin and delicate, yet energetic for all that. "She broke her neck."

Geraldine Prather touched a hand to her mouth. "Poor man. To lose his wife in such a senseless way. But there's no right way to lose someone, is there? I've always thought the stairs in these homes were rather steep. I'm always careful to hold on to the bannister, and I have pretty good balance. I used to be a dancer."

Rex smiled and gestured to her footwear. "I noticed the ballet shoes."

"I always wear flats, out of habit." She smiled in turn, much recovered, it seemed, from when he had first arrived. "You know, I find it reassuring that you're staying in Notting Hamlet. You have a very reassuring presence." She smiled again. "I'm not saying the police haven't been very thorough, but I have difficulty believing it was that house agent. Everyone I've spoken to says he's their main suspect. But I expect the police have to produce somebody to prove they're doing their job."

"Murder cases can take time. If the police have insufficient evidence against Chris Walker to charge him, they have to release him within ninety-six hours, and they have to make a special application to detain him that long. But they'll keep him under close surveillance if they still suspect him of the murders."

Geraldine shook back her tight copper curls. "I don't know what to think. I just don't see what motive he would have had," she said with puzzlement in her voice. "And he didn't strike me as a particularly shady character on the few occasions I spoke with him. Will you let me know as soon as you find out anything concrete?" She stared at Rex over her coffee cup, a worried look in her eyes. "Do you think it's safe to stay here?"

"I can't really advise either way. If I were you, though, I would consider getting away for a while, if only to avoid the stress of the situation."

"I have been thinking about taking a holiday," Geraldine said. "I've always wanted to go to Thailand."

"Do you know Charlotte Spelling up the street? She runs a travel business called Get Up and Go, which I believe caters to last-minute bookings. I have her number, if you'd like it."

"I would indeed. Thank you. It seems like divine providence." Geraldine set down her cup and tapped her knees. "Bangkok, here I come!"

Rex declined her offer of more coffee and they exchanged numbers. As he left, he promised to keep in touch.

The walk back to Malcolm's house helped to clear his head, which was a hive of mental activity, his thoughts buzzing to and fro and always returning to the central theme of proving who had committed the murders—all five of them. For he had little doubt they were related.

EIGHTEEN

REX RETURNED FROM GERALDINE Prather's house to find Malcolm, trowel in hand, crouched by the shrubbery between the garage and front door.

"I'm about ready to come in," his friend said, glancing up from his work. "Will Welsh rarebit and salad do you for lunch?"

"Perfect." Miss Bird had made grated cheese on toast for Rex when he was a boy, and it had remained a firm favourite.

"Put the kettle on, will you? I'll be in in a jiffy. Can't wait to hear what's new."

"How do you know I came up with anything new?" Rex asked in amusement, pausing on the path.

Malcolm rested his right arm on his knee, the trowel dangling from his hand. "You have that expectant look, as though you've come by a new piece of evidence."

"Most of my evidence, as you call it, has been hearsay. But you are not wrong." Rex spied Mr. Prendergast hovering in his front garden and called out a greeting to alert Malcolm of his presence, so his friend would not blurt out anything about the case, which might then travel around Notting Hamlet.

He spun on his heel and proceeded to the front door. Inside the hall, he shed his outer garments and went to the kitchen to start the tea as Malcolm had directed. His laptop and notepad lay on the oak veneer table where he had left them earlier that morning. Upon sitting down, he committed to paper what Danny had told him.

Malcolm entered the room while he was still writing. "Well, let's have it," he said, turning on the sink faucet. He squeezed a plastic bottle of dish soap on his hands and started methodically scrubbing his nails with a brush.

"I spoke to the newspaper lad," Rex informed his friend.

"Danny? Shifty sort of boy, but a wizard on that bike."

"Aye, he did manage to extort thirty pounds from me." Rex repeated Danny's account of the old man in the back of the BMW.

"And you believe him?"

"The details were very specific and tied in with what Lottie said. I'm thinking the Russian couple were in that car with him. Charlotte's description of them suggests similarly flamboyant characters. The young woman was wearing a fur coat, and now we have an old man with a *shapka* on his head."

"Did you see Charlotte?" Malcolm asked, drying his hands on a dishtowel.

"No, but I spoke to Geraldine Prather again, the lady who met John Calpin. The poor woman was visibly affected by the news of his death. She said she was thinking of going on holiday to Thailand, and I gave her Charlotte's number."

"Good thinking. Was Geraldine able to tell you anything more?"

"No, we just chatted for a while over coffee."

"So what now?" Malcolm opened the refrigerator and took out a block of cheddar cheese.

"How d'you fancy a trip to Luton?"

"Luton? Not on your neillie. I haven't been further than Godminton since ... I don't know when."

"Since Jocelyn's death. Malcolm, you're becoming a hermit."

"Why d'you want to go to Luton? Or Lu'n, as they call it there."

A large town and borough of Bedfordshire, Luton lay thirty miles north of London. Rex had flown out of its international airport on several occasions.

"Penworth Press, Calpin's publisher, is based there." Rex consulted his notes. "On Reginald Road. I thought I'd try to make an appointment with his editor tomorrow."

"Why not just speak on the phone?"

"I'm hoping to get hold of some of Calpin's manuscript or material. He must have submitted a proposal to get the book deal. And I'm assuming he supplied his editor with chapters as the book progressed. His subject matter was the Cruikshank gang, among others, and I may be able to offer the editor a *quid pro quo* based on what I know."

"Which is what, exactly?" Malcolm produced a cheese grater from a drawer and set to work.

"Who might've murdered John Calpin. It would make for a more saleable book, from the publisher's point of view." Rex sat back in his chair, a pencil see-sawing between his fingers. "And I could furnish details on the Cruikshank family gleaned from what I've heard from residents here. It's worth a try."

He paused while he arranged his thoughts in logical order. "Calpin was writing a book on a mobster family who disappeared in the mid-nineties. He came to Notting Hamlet under the pretence of looking for his birth mother. It's possible Valerie Trotter was his birth mother, but I doubt it. If you discovered your mother was part of a reviled mob under the scrutiny of every law enforcement agency in the land, would you want to be associated with her?"

"If I was a budding young journalist, I might use it to my advantage," Malcolm replied. "Perhaps his editor will be able to enlighten you."

"Perhaps. I wonder how Calpin found the four of them. They seem to have created very elaborate identities."

"Judging by that photo you showed me of Sylvia Cruikshank," Malcolm said from where he stood at the counter, "Valerie Trotter went for a complete makeover. From brunette to blonde with a new set of thingummies. And no more librarian glasses. I wouldn't have recognized her if she was my own sister."

"I wonder if Ernest's arthritis was a sham," Rex wondered aloud. "Not to mention his weak heart and Alzheimer's. This was the man who used to be known as Kevlar Kev. Then there was Barry's hearing aid. A useful ploy if you want to pretend not to hear inopportune questions." He cupped a hand to his ear. "Whaat's that you say?" he asked in a quavering voice. "And Vic Chandler's fear of heights, and him chief enforcer for one of England's most dangerous gangs! They did a fine job of making themselves oot to be a bunch of frail geriatrics, wimps, and vacuous blondes."

"Ernest and Barry were getting on," Malcolm reminded him. "Even mobsters have to retire. I suppose we should call them Kev and Frankie now."

"It must be them," Rex said, clenching his pencil in his fist. "I made a note of Kev and Frankie's birthdate," he added, flipping back the pages of his pad. "Ernest and Barry were reported in the media as being two years apart. That can't be correct if they were twins."

"They'd have wanted to conceal that fact to further protect their identity," Malcolm said.

"And since they were fraternal twins and not identical, or even the same height, that wouldn't have posed a problem. I wonder which poor stiffs they stole their identities from."

"They'll be long buried under a pile of concrete," Malcolm said. "Or else fed a lot of fish somewhere off the Essex coast." Inured though he was to blood and dissection, the doctor gave an exaggerated shudder.

Rex stopped flipping back and forth in his pad when he found the twins' birthdate. "They would have been eighty-two. Kev shaved a year off his age, and Frankie three."

"Wish I could."

"In any case, looks like their cover was blown by John Calpin, who also ended up dead at the hands of their old arch enemies. The editor's got to think that'll sell copies." Rex paused. "There's conflicting information as to whether Ivan's gang was Russian or Ukrainian."

"Same difference."

"Not necessarily to them," Rex pointed out.

"All I know is they have names like Petrov and Vasili, and talk with menacing accents. These corrupt commies infiltrate everywhere. I hope I never have to come face-to-face with one."

Malcolm's limited worldview reflected Rick Ballantine's. "I'd say these people were capitalists, into whatever markets they could exploit," Rex said. "For all I know, they might still be in business."

"Other than the assassination business, you mean."

They continued their speculation over lunch, after which Malcolm cleared the table. Donning a pair of rubber gloves, he cleaned the non-dishwasher safe items in the sink. Rex organized his legal documents on the table. He had brought the briefs with him from chambers to work on over his long weekend away.

"You can use my study," Malcolm said, peeling off the yellow gloves. "It's not as though I use it much anymore, though I have been thinking of applying for a forensic pathologist job I heard about. Working on this case has reawakened my interest. Not that I've been much use to you…"

"Nonsense," Rex contradicted kindly. "And it's grand you're thinking of getting back in the field." Three years was too long to mooch about the house, he thought. It wasn't healthy. "And thanks for the offer of your study, but I've grown accustomed to working here at the table."

"Right-oh. Well, I'll be in the garage sorting through some old stuff if you need me. And I thought we'd go to *Ciao's* this evening. They do divine calamari and chicken alfredo."

"Perfect. And maybe a pint at the King's Head afterwards. Incidentally, why do Bedfordshire natives refer to themselves as Clangers?" Rex asked, recalling his conversation with Malcolm's neighbour, Win Prendergast.

"The term derives from a traditional Beds suet pastry by that name, which is half filled with meat and half with jam."

"Funny it's not on the pub menu," Rex said with a grimace.

Malcolm grinned back, and Rex felt their old friendship re-cementing after he had raked him over the coals for his acts of naïve stupidity in the case.

Malcolm left him to his work and Rex absorbed himself in it without further prevarication. The prospect of dining out at the Italian restaurant in Godminton spurned him on, especially as he did not relish another evening in the house. Much as he felt at home in Malcolm's kitchen, it could do with some remodelling, he mused briefly, before throwing himself back into his court documents for the next two hours. An imminent case at the High Court of Justiciary involved a domestic dispute, where he was tasked to prove that the husband had suffocated his cheating wife. Finishing sooner than anticipated, he returned to the more fascinating case of the Notting Hamlet murders. At that moment the phone rang. He called out for Malcolm and, getting no response, went to answer it himself.

"It's Charlotte," the voice said. "How are things going?"

"I've been taking a short break from our local murders to work on a couple of court cases." Charlotte made a sympathetic noise at her end. "Shall I get Malcolm?" he asked.

"Actually, it's you I wanted to talk to. Geraldine Prather asked me to arrange her trip to the Far East. Thank you for referring her to me. We met this afternoon and I was able to get her a terrific package deal."

"I wish you could get away, too."

"No chance of that. How long are you sticking around?"

"Until Tuesday."

"Hope I see you before you leave. What's Malcolm up to?"

"Rummaging in the garage. He's been more active and cheerful lately, which I put down to you."

"And you, he told me."

"All right, I'll take some of the credit too," Rex said with a laugh.

A nice woman, he thought, walking back to the kitchen after the call. He hoped it worked out between her and Malcolm. His friend was just entering from the laundry room, looking dishevelled.

"I just got off the phone with Charlotte," Rex told him.

"Oh. What did she want?"

"To thank me for putting her in contact with Geraldine and to see what you were doing."

Malcolm gave a pleased smile. "Well, I've made quite a dent, actually. I have a couple of boxes for Oxfam. Your Mrs. Jensen will be pleased."

"Did you throw in your balaclava?" Rex joked.

"It's back under the stairs, retired from night duty. Right, I'll go clean myself up. Will you be ready to leave in half an hour?"

The doorbell rang just then. Malcolm checked his watch. "I wonder who that could be." He went to look through the peephole and returned from the front door wearing a wary expression.

NINETEEN

"It's that biker, Big Bill. What should we do?" Malcolm asked, wringing his hands.

Rex suppressed a sigh, realizing that Malcolm, of his own volition, would not open the door to the visitor. "I'll get it and make my excuses for you."

"Say I'm in the shower. Don't let him in."

Rex strode to the front door and swung it open. Eye to eye with him stood the biker, his tall frame lean and muscular, and clad in supple black leather. He wore an unbuckled helmet covered in stickers and sported a greying blonde beard that outdid Rex's in sheer volume.

"You the barrister from Edinburgh?" the man boomed.

"Guilty as charged."

"Bill Little." Hence the ironic nickname, Rex thought; though Big Bill's actual size would have been enough to merit it.

"What can I do for you, Mr. Little?" Rex guessed Danny had given his uncle his business card, but he didn't suppose this was a purely friendly visit.

"You spoke to my boy."

"I did. And he was amply compensated for it."

The man grinned beneath his walrus moustache, displaying a perfect set of teeth. "Good, because I too have some information that might interest you." He spoke with perfect diction, though his speech was slurred through laziness, or possibly drink or weed.

Danny had clearly inherited his uncle's eye for the main chance. "Very kind of you to bring it to me," Rex told Big Bill. "I'd invite you in, but it's not my house." He imagined Malcolm cowering at the top of the stairs, listening with rapt attention.

Big Bill waved away his concern. He would not feel the cold in his biker gear, Rex thought, but he himself would if he stepped outside. He should close the door to prevent the warm air from escaping, even if it meant Malcolm would no longer be able to hear the exchange. Torn between what to do, he decided to accelerate the conversation.

"I was getting ready to leave the house, but if it'll just take a minute," he prompted.

The biker removed his helmet in one swift motion, releasing a shock of tawny hair much like his nephew's, only shoulder-length and streaked with silver. "It concerns a false alibi."

Rex considered the information. "Whose? There are only two police suspects so far—correct me if I'm wrong. And one of them doesn't have an alibi. That leaves the handyman who lives on your street."

Smoky blue eyes, crinkled at the outer corners, held Rex's gaze. "Mr. Graves, I was a Bond Street broker before the stock market crashed in 20008 and I don't believe in wasting time. Yes, Randall Gomez is the suspect I refer to."

"Ex-suspect, I believe."

"Well, maybe not."

"I won't waste your time either," Rex said. "How much are you asking?"

"A hundred quid. My nephew and I had a good life in the City, but times have changed. I'm not too proud to ask for what I can get."

"But as a stockbroker, you'll understand the value of money better than most."

"I understand it can evaporate in a New York nanosecond."

"I'm not sure your information is worth anything to me," Rex stated. "Gomez is not on my suspect list, regardless of whether his alibi stands up or not."

Big Bill bowed his head and sighed in resignation.

"Have you taken your information to the police?" Rex enquired.

"No, and I don't intend to. Anyway, from what I gather, you may be making more headway than them in the case."

"If I am it's because certain individuals have not been particularly forthcoming with the authorities. I'll give you fifty if what you know is valid and first-hand."

"I saw it for myself." Big Bill waited and Rex nodded for him to continue. "Gomez was outside Valerie Trotter's house at lunchtime the day of the murders ringing on the bell. I'm sure he has a key, because they, well, you know ... but he scarpered when he heard my bike."

"I'm told it's extremely loud. He would have heard you before you turned onto Fox Lane."

"That's as may be, but he acted suspiciously and hurried away from the door."

"You actually saw him ring the bell? And you're sure it was him?"

"His arm was held out and up. Like this." Big Bill gave a demonstration. The jacket sleeve rode down his forearm revealing a plethora of tattoos. "And yes, it was definitely him. Plus, his van was there."

"He may have lied to the police simply because he didn't want to reveal the full nature of his relationship with Ms. Trotter, for fear they'd think he'd tracked her down at Mr. Blackwell's and killed her in a jealous rage."

"For seeing that bald bull-neck?" Big Bill suggested.

So the biker knew about her relationship with Vic Chandler, the ex-enforcer for the Cruikshank Twins. Evidently, the pair had not been careful enough.

Rex extracted his wallet from his trouser pocket and slid out the money promised. "Your nephew's information was more valuable, but I'll follow up on yours, too."

"Danny wouldn't have made that up about the old man in the BMW. He doesn't have that kind of imagination."

"Any chance you know the name of the nursing home in Bedford, which Mr. Gomez was supposed to be visiting the day of the murders?"

"Sunnyview. Something like that. He said it was one of the nicer ones. It's this side of Bedford."

Rex handed over the fifty-pound note. "Sorry to hear you lost your lucrative position."

"Ah, well. It was a rat race. Better off out of it in some ways." Big Bill held up the cash between two ringed fingers in a gesture of thanks and walked down the path to his orange, polished chrome Harley Davidson 2000cc, pulling the helmet back on his head.

Rex closed the front door. "Sorry to let oot the central heating," he called up to Malcolm, "but I thought you'd want to listen in."

Malcolm came halfway down the stairs and leaned on the bannister. "Sounds like you got scammed."

"His information was solid enough, if not very useful. I decided fifty pounds was worth it to keep the peace between you and your biker friends."

"Too kind. I didn't know he was a stockbroker. Not quite the rabble-rouser I thought he was." Malcolm turned back up the stairs and promised to be quick in the shower.

Rex returned to the kitchen and reached inside the refrigerator for a Guinness. Seated in front of his laptop, he researched nursing homes in Bedford and found one by the name of Sunnyvale, which was close enough to "Sunnyview," the name Big Bill had given him, and it was in the right location. He would check out Handy Randy's alibi on his way to Luton, just to be sure.

TWENTY

Preoccupied by intermingling thoughts of the case and of his fiancée, now on the second full day of her cruise, Rex exited off the A1 onto the A421 towards Bedford, thereafter planning to get onto the M1 to Luton. He had little trouble finding the nursing home, whose website had given directions to a street on the outskirts of Bedford. Even though Rex did not expect to learn much, except perhaps to verify the driving distance between Notting Hamlet and Sunnyvale, it was only a minor detour, and any lead, even those eliminated by the police, was worth checking out, in his estimation.

The street housed large residences of the pre-war era surrounded by generous grounds, for the most part walled in and containing an array of mature native trees. Such was the case with Sunnyvale, which had, in addition, two modern annexes extending from either side of the main structure. Built in brick with a pebbledash upper floor punctuated with large white-framed bay windows, its front overlooked a courtyard.

Crossing the redbrick pavers arranged in a herringbone pattern around flowerbeds and wooden benches, Rex reached the main entrance, a glass doorway wide enough to accommodate wheelchairs for the old and infirm.

As soon as he walked inside, an odour of disinfectant overlaying that of catheters assailed him, much as an obvious attempt had been made with the decor and furnishings to conceal the institutional nature of Sunnyvale and to preserve the illusion of a large, comfortable home.

"Good morning. May I assist you?" demanded a young woman in a powder blue uniform dress.

"I've come to visit Mrs. Gomez." Rex was banking on the fact that Randall's mother shared the same surname. In any case, there could not be more than twenty beds in the home, and she could be located easily enough.

"I'll take you to Matron. Please come with me."

Passing an old man holding onto a walking frame, Rex followed her down a short, carpeted corridor off the lobby to a door bearing the name "Barbara Henshaw, RGN."

"A visitor for Marta," the nursing assistant told the stout woman in starched white seated behind a well-organized mahogany desk. The matron thanked her and she left.

"Please." In a forthright and pleasant manner, Barbara Henshaw indicated one of two armchairs in front of her desk. An online photo of the owner of Sunnyvale had faithfully represented her abundance of stiff grey hair and cherubic cheeks.

"Rex Graves," he introduced himself.

"Marta is at the hospital this morning. Nothing serious," the matron hastened to add. "Some routine tests. Have you come far?"

"From Notting Hamlet. I'm acquainted with her son, Randall Gomez."

"I'm afraid she won't be back for at least another hour. Would you care to wait?"

"Unfortunately I have an appointment in Luton. How is she?"

"Her moments of lucidity are becoming few and far between," the matron replied matter-of-factly. "She's extremely frail and dependent on staff for most of her care." Barbara Henshaw opened a file. "Randall made sure his mother was assigned one of our very best rooms. It has a lovely view over the pond at the back. She spends much of her time at the window."

Rex noticed a brochure in the folder. "Marbella," he said in surprise.

"She owns a timeshare there. Randall says he might have found a buyer. This was a month ago and the next bill for his mother's care is due. Are you related at all?" The matron looked at Rex in his nice overcoat as though she would have liked to ask him to foot the expense.

"No, just a casual acquaintance."

She sighed. "I don't suppose a timeshare in Marbella appeals?" she asked with a coy smile.

"I'm not one for hot weather," Rex demurred.

"You may change your mind when you're old and feel the cold more. Randall said the condo was a very sound investment."

Rex refrained from suggesting she consider it for herself. "Och, well, perhaps I can come back," he said, rising from his chair. "When is the best time to visit?"

"Mornings generally. Marta sleeps away most of the afternoon." Barbara Henshaw stood and reached across the desk to shake hands.

"It was good to meet you, Mr. Graves. I'll tell Marta you came. Don't forget to sign our visitors' book."

Rex found it in the lobby and did so in his most illegible scrawl. As he was moving away from the table, he noticed an old woman bundled in a wheelchair, drooling with a vacant stare, her face as pale and crepey as parchment. The girl in blue came to whisk her away wordlessly to one of the annexes.

Heartsick at the prospect of one day putting his aging mother in a home, Rex was glad to regain the fresh air of the deserted courtyard. His brief visit had, however, served some purpose. Marta Gomez might not have been alert enough to notice her son's disappearance, nor might the staff, judging by the lack of activity in the lobby, especially if the patient's room was upstairs and at the back—where there might well be a service entrance, as was typical in these old homes. Rex walked around one of the wings and found there was, and that it was locked from the outside.

Of equal interest was the timeshare brochure. He pondered this discovery as he retrieved his car and started on the route that would take him to the M1. This might be a duplicate of the brochure found on Ernest Blackwell's corpse. Randall Gomez had been the deceased's handyman. Had Ernest, the old Kev, been planning to move to Marbella? The Costa del Sol was overrun by retired Brits. It was the Florida of Spain, from what Rex had seen of the state. He supposed Marbella was as good a place as any to hide out, and certainly warmer than Bedfordshire.

Roadworks near Cranfield caused a disruption in the flow of traffic, but he had allowed plenty of time, and once on the motorway he encountered no further delays. By 11:15, he was on Reginald Road looking out for Penworth Press, and spotted the large brass plaque a split second before he passed it. Turning sharply, he found a fortuitous parking spot outside the building and gathered his briefcase and phone. Seeing that Malcolm had called, and with fifteen minutes to spare before his appointment with Ken Penworth, he returned the call, thinking it must be important if his friend was trying to reach him. Malcolm was not the sort of person to phone for an idle chat.

"Where are you?" his friend asked.

"Outside Penworth Press, a respectable-looking establishment in lovely Luton."

"Did you visit the nursing home?"

"Aye, but Marta Gomez wasn't there. I spoke to the matron. From what I gathered, it's quite possible the son returned to Notting Hamlet undetected. But I think Randall's intentions were more amorous than murderous, and when he found Valerie Trotter wasn't home, returned to his mother's bedside. There was a brochure in her file featuring a timeshare in Marbella, such as you found tucked inside Ernest Blackwell's waistband."

"A Spanish connection, eh? But what about the Russian connection? Isn't this fun? International espionage!"

"Hopefully my meeting with this editor will help clarify a few things. What's happening at your end?"

"I was filling in my job application. The reason I called is Lottie phoned with further news about the poisoning."

"Poisoning?"

"The loud dog at forty-seven."

Rex had almost forgotten about that particular situation. "Do we know who did it?"

"As good as. The vet found thallium nitrate in the poor mutt. Perhaps there was excess shedding that alerted him to it. It's a lethal drug a chemistry teacher would have no difficulty administering in the appropriate dose to quieten the dog forever. Could've put it in its water bowl, since it's colourless, odourless, and tasteless."

"But would Mr. Woods have ready access to thallium nitrate?"

"Perhaps he used it in school experiments. Who knows? Anyway, might be something or nothing, to quote Lottie. I wanted to let you know in case it had any bearing in your investigation. Oh, that's the door. I'd better get it. Good luck with Penworth." Malcolm cut the connection.

Rex compared the time on both dashboard and phone and got out of the car. A jetliner soared overhead in the cloudy grey sky, temporarily eclipsing the sound of traffic, and he thought wistfully of Helen on her eight-day cruise. He climbed the polished stone steps leading into the premises of Penworth Press, where the receptionist phoned through to the grandson of the founder of the publishing house, the editor he was due to meet. Hopefully, he would get the answers he needed.

TWENTY-ONE

"Thank you for fitting me in at such short notice," Rex said upon being introduced to Ken Penworth in his narrow, book-crammed office on the second floor.

"My pleasure. What you said on the phone was most intriguing." Mr. Penworth looked older than his voice, which was high-pitched and eager, and moreover, did not match his obese frame. "Let me take your coat. Do sit yourself down. I believe you mentioned you were a Scottish advocate?" Settling into his executive chair, he beamed at Rex.

Rex acknowledged he was and provided enough inside information about the Notting Hamlet murders and John Calpin's visit to the community to be viewed as a credible source. "Did you know Mr. Calpin had visited Notting Hamlet?" he asked the editor.

"Not specifically. He said he'd tracked the Cruikshank gang to somewhere in Bedfordshire. How, I don't know. But your account of how he told the resident he was seeking his birth mother shows just how resourceful a journalist he was. John had a good nose. I was waiting on the next batch of pages concerning the gang's new identities, which he'd promised to send me the week he disappeared. His laptop is presumably sitting in some lab in Glasgow now, and those crucial pages with it."

Rex thought it probable there was little, if anything, left of a computer, let alone its files, judging by what had happened to its owner. All research into the Russian gang would likely have been destroyed along with John Calpin.

"It's all very frustrating," the editor went on. "But perhaps you can help fill in the gaps."

"I've brought my notes. I'm afraid they're in longhand. I'll be giving the police a set too, of course."

"Of course," Ken Penworth said, glancing at Rex's briefcase as though he wanted to eat it. "What is it you'd like to know from me?" he pre-empted. "I assume that's why you're here. Unless you're looking for a book deal?" he asked with an unctuous smile.

"Heavens, no. I'm just looking for some answers. Well, confirmation, really. A friend of mine who lives in Notting Hamlet asked me to look into the case. My focus was on those murders before I ever heard of John Calpin."

The editor tapped his desk decisively. "I knew your name seemed familiar! I remember now. The Christmas murders in Sussex?"

"At Swanmere Manor."

"That's right! Fascinating." Ken Penworth buzzed an assistant and said to hold his calls for an hour. "And send up sandwiches and coffee for two. Ham and cheese?" he asked Rex, who nodded and thanked him. The editor repeated the order into the intercom and released the button.

While waiting for lunch, the two men discussed the two current cases, merging and meshing information. Rex outlined his theory about how the Cruikshank twins had retired with Kev's daughter to the secluded community of Notting Hamlet on their ill-gotten gains, bringing their minder with them. Kev's wife, he'd discovered in the course of his research, had died of natural causes. A second daughter had disassociated herself from the family and married a house painter. The felonious members of the gang had buried their old identities and forged new ones. "John was on to them long before I was," Rex concluded.

"I'd heard on the news about the Notting Hamlet murders, of course," Ken Penworth said. "But I never made the connection to John's work. But then I'm no detective," he added with a fatuous smile. "And all four identities can be confirmed?"

"Almost certainly. Face recognition software might help confirm Valerie's true identity failing all else. A comparison between an old newspaper photograph of Sylvia Cruikshank and a more recent one of Valerie Trotter shows a passing resemblance at best. She changed her hair colour and bust size, and did away with her glasses. But Valerie was working as a bookkeeper, Sylvia's old job. I doubt the police found any evidence of their old identities in their homes. It appears they were very careful."

No doubt they had forged passports to go with their assumed names, Rex thought, suspecting that Kev, at least, had been planning to use his to move to Spain. Randall Gomez might know more about that.

The editor nodded periodically as he jotted down notes. "This is likely what would have been in the instalment I was waiting for from John. I imagine his killer cottoned on to what he was doing and decided to stop him before he spilled the beans."

"And to stop anybody else who got a similar idea, judging by the mutilation of his body. It was clearly a warning to other journalists, a blatant threat if ever I saw one. And I've seen a few in the course of my legal career."

"Against yourself?"

"Fortunately, no. At least, nothing major. Not yet."

A bespectacled young man brought in their cellophane-wrapped sandwiches and bistro containers of coffee. Ken Penworth cleared a space on the desk and stuck a paper napkin into his collar, covering the top half of his saffron yellow tie. Rex felt he had divulged adequate information on his side. What he sought, he told the editor once the assistant had left, was background information on the rival Russian gang and what might have prompted the murders at Notting Hamlet after an intervening period of almost two decades.

Penworth poured a sachet of sugar into his cup. "I suppose we should go back to just before the Cruikshanks and their enforcer disappeared, as we all thought, to Australia. If the Russian gang was simply putting a frightener on them by posting that firebomb through the letter box, the Cruikshanks took it seriously and retaliated by murdering four members of the Dragunov family, including Ivan's eldest son. The twins, accused of masterminding the attack, were never convicted, due to insufficient evidence and intimidation of witnesses, but they must have realized their days were numbered if they didn't vanish, and soon. The nephew, Darrell Cruikshank, had already been put away. If the law didn't catch up with them one day, they knew the MIR gang would. John lays it all out in his book."

Rex, who had been chewing on his sandwich, was thrilled to hear the editor name the gang. He pronounced it as the Russians would, with a prolonged "e" in the middle. Rex hadn't told Ken Penworth about the letters written in blood on the Notting Hamlet victims, and perhaps even on John Calpin's forehead. "I read there was a Russian outfit operating by that name," he told Penworth, "but I didn't yet know about the murder of the Dragunov family members by the Cruikshank gang. So Ivan the Terrible was searching for them all this time?"

"It's a question of honour," Ken Penworth explained. "Gang retribution has no statute of limitations. You don't leave a wrong committed against your family un-righted, especially your immediate family, however long ago it happened. Ivan lost a brother, two nephews, and a son who would have been his successor."

"An eye for an eye," Rex said and took a gulp of coffee. "Four hits for four murders. How did the Russians die? And who were they?"

"They were originally from the Moscow suburbs. But some of Ivan's distant relatives live in Eastern Ukraine. A bomb was placed in the undercarriage of the family Mercedes while they were attending a Russian Orthodox wedding in London. Ivan, his wife, and the younger children were travelling in a separate vehicle. The bomb was thought to have been made and planted by Fred the Spanner. He learnt about explosives in the army. The bomb blew the Mercedes to smithereens the moment the ignition was turned. Nobody got out alive and several people standing close by were injured. It was a very thorough job. John described the whole scene. He had a deft way of fictionalizing fact that brought the pages alive. The book is a gripping read from start to finish."

"So it's pretty much completed?" Rex asked.

"Almost. He was doing some more fact-checking, and much of the manuscript reads like a first draft, but that's what editors are for," Mr. Penworth said with smug satisfaction. "It will end up being a more relevant story now, showing the MIR gang is still a force to be reckoned with. The information you provided will tie it up nicely. We shall, of course, list you in the acknowledgments. And perhaps we can come to some financial arrangement? After all, without you, we might never have discovered where precisely the Cruikshank gang ended their days and who murdered them and John."

Rex raised his hands, pushing out with his palms. "Thanks, but no." He didn't want to profit from the journalist's untimely death. "I'd rather keep my anonymity," he told the editor. "And not become a target myself."

"I understand." Ken Penworth proceeded to look aggrieved. "Yes, it's a shame to have to publish the work posthumously, but it's what John would have wished. He wouldn't have wanted to die in vain."

The two men tied up loose ends over the rest of lunch. Ken Penworth dabbed at his mouth with his paper bib and removed it from his collar. He buzzed in his assistant and gave him Rex's notes to photocopy, assuring the Scotsman that none of the information would be leaked before Rex had time to take it to the police and have it confirmed. Rex did not know if they had yet connected the Notting Hamlet murders to the MIR gang and back to Calpin's abduction and killing.

In exchange, Penworth printed off from his computer the chapters from John Calpin's book relevant to Rex's investigation, with a reminder that the material was copyrighted. Documents were signed and the business concluded. Rex had obtained what he had come for, and Penworth Press now possessed the missing pieces to make *Baddest British Mobsters* whole.

"I'll have to summon my ghost-writing skills," the editor joked. "Unless the police send over the rest of the manuscript before the book goes to print. In any case, fear not—I won't divulge my source."

Reassured on that point, Rex left the publishing house and set out on his return trip to Notting Hamlet, making a brief stop for gas before he got on the M1. It was from that point he began to notice a black Jaguar in his rear view mirror and fear he might be being followed.

TWENTY-TWO

THE BLACK JAGUAR SEDAN, maintaining an inconspicuous distance, exited the motorway and turned, and then slowed down and sped up whenever Rex did. Perhaps he was being paranoid, he thought, even as he reflected how the shiny front grille badge had taken on a sinister aspect in his rear view mirror. He called Malcolm on both his home number and mobile, and receiving no answer, left brief messages urging him to get back to him as soon as possible.

By the time he reached Notting Hamlet by a deliberately circuitous route along lonely country lanes, he felt reasonably certain he had shed his tail. He even began to doubt there had been one in the first place and was already laughing to himself in anticipation of sharing his experience with Malcolm as he walked in the front door. He called out for his friend. No answer.

Failing to locate him in the kitchen, he went through to the garage and saw his car was there. He peeked into the living room and then went to the study, where Malcolm would have been working on his application. He found the desk strewn with periodicals and papers, a tea mug knocked over, and the contents spilt on a document. Rex ran upstairs and searched all the rooms. Where was he?

The last thing Malcolm had said on the phone, as Rex recalled, was that he needed to answer the door. The implication of that in light of the murders in Notting Hamlet filled him with panic and dread.

Frantically, he checked the yard. No gardening tools lay about, nothing to suggest his friend had been there that morning. What would account for his car being in the garage and for his leaving the front door unlocked in his absence? Why hadn't Malcolm called him back?

As Rex returned to the kitchen from outside, his eyes adjusting to the gloom after the broad daylight, a movement to his right by the laundry room door caught his eye.

"Oh, there you are." But even as he said it, he realized the man in the cheap jeans and lime green nylon jacket was not Malcolm. Rex stopped mid-stride, his body instinctively rigid with fear. Metal glinted in the intruder's hand. Of similar height to Malcolm, and likewise grey-haired, he was more flaccid in build. As the man's features crystallized, they assumed a faint familiarity, but Rex at that moment could not place them. "Who are you and what are you doing here?" he demanded in a hoarse voice.

"I'd ask you the same, 'cept I already know." The man's voice had a flat, nasal quality.

"I'm a guest in this house," Rex responded. "Which you, patently, are not. Where's the owner? What have you done with him?"

The man glanced down at his butcher's knife. Rex felt the bile rise in his throat, but found he could not move his muscles. He had a vision of Malcolm's body crumpled under the stairs. His paralysis dissipated. Involuntarily, he looked towards the hall. The man sprang, cornering him between the back door and kitchen counter. Escape was impossible. The armed man would be on top of him before he could get out the door. Though shorter, he was more agile. A grim expression haunted the pale eyes. Rex had seen that wary, soulless expression enough times to know the man had spent time in prison. The pallid skin deprived of adequate sun and fresh air confirmed his impression. And now Rex knew who was standing before him wielding the knife, and yet was at a loss to understand why.

"You're Darrell Cruikshank." The man had only been out of prison a month, as Rex had confirmed from a call to Belmarsh; barely enough time to acclimatize to the twenty-first century after two decades of incarceration.

"Oh, you definitely need to go, Mr. Graves," the ex-con said in a grating voice. His thin lips curled around chipped, nicotine-stained teeth. "You know far too much for your own good."

He approached in a smooth movement, his sneakers squeaking on the linoleum floor. His knife pointed to a chair at the kitchen table. "Sit here and give us your phone."

Seeing no option, Rex relinquished it and sat down, his back to the kitchen door and to the man, whose body at close quarters gave off a sour aroma of sweat. He heard the door lock behind him. He made an effort to control his breathing and clear his brain as he tried to ascertain the significance of Kev and Frankie's nephew ambushing him in Malcolm's home.

"Why are you threatening me, Mr. Cruikshank? And why did you have to do away with Malcolm Patterson? I came to Notting Hamlet to help discover who murdered your family."

"You had no business sticking your nose in."

"I wanted to seek justice for the four victims. The fact that I now know who they really were hasn't changed anything. As far as I'm aware, they lived the last twenty years as law-abiding citizens."

"Free."

"Excuse me?"

"Free. While I wasted twenty of my best years inside. I'm fifty-seven now, used up and out of touch. It's like I landed on another planet. Nothing feels the same. Even the people are different."

"It must be hard on you that your family's gone."

"What you talking about? My uncles and cousin never came to visit me in the joint, not once."

"They were supposed to be in Australia."

"Not even a card. Uncle Kev got away with murder, including the hit on Ivan's family, and Fred received a light sentence for smashing a bottle in somebody's face, while I got twenty for white collar crime. Different lawyer, see. Kev and Barry could have hauled Wiggins's arse back from his holiday villa in Ibiza, but I s'ppose I wasn't worth the trouble. I was expendable." Darrell split the word into four distinct syllables. "Well, I showed them. The chloroform made Kev a bit woozy, but he knew what I was planning to do with that piano wire. Pure terror in his voice when he said, 'Dar, you wouldn't do this to your old uncle, would ya?' Too right, I would. I did what I dreamt of every night for two decades."

Rex found himself temporarily speechless. "It was you?" he uttered at last. This man was not on his side, at all.

"You never figured that out?" goaded the voice in his ear. "I thought you were some big-name private detective."

"I failed to see a motive."

"Motive!" the man sneered. "They left me to rot behind bars all those years. How 'bout that for motive? I never squealed on them even though it would have meant a lesser sentence. They owed me so much more than half a mil. That's nothing today, and I been inside too long to start over." He spoke with cold fury. "That's not all, neither." The man spat on Malcolm's clean floor and paused. Rex felt sure Cruikshank would use the blade on him then. "Soon as they sold their homes, I knew I'd never find them again, or my dough."

"I thought a young Russian couple was responsible for the four murders," Rex said in an effort to prolong the conversation and his life.

"Igor and Svetlana? Nah, they were just casing the community. They're Ivan's youngest son and daughter. I did the dirty work in exchange for securing my future."

"So you defected to the Russians?"

"I wouldn't put it quite like that, Rex, me old pal. Anyway, they signalled you'd be here. Where's your briefcase?"

"In the hall." Rex hoped Cruikshank would be stupid enough to fetch it, giving him an opportunity to escape through the kitchen door.

"It can stay there till they arrive."

"Who?" Rex asked.

"The people who followed you on the motorway. Ivan and his driver. You shouldn't have gone to Luton, Rex. The editor at Penworth Press will meet with an unfortunate accident when he drives home from work."

"I suppose you had plenty of practice with those ice cream vans."

"I see you've been doing your homework." Cruikshank clapped slowly.

Rex twisted his head round far enough to see that the man had his thumb hooked around the knife handle. "Why don't you just finish me off right now," he said with bravado, "instead of making me sit here."

"We're waiting on the Czar." Rex detected agitation in Cruikshank's voice. "It's so quiet here. I'll never get used to the quiet after where I been."

"Your friends should be here by now," Rex remarked a moment later. "Unless they got lost, or else hit a pothole. The roads around here are so badly signed and maintained it's a good possibility."

"I didn't ask your opinion, so just shut up, okay?"

In the ensuing silence, punctuated only by the ticking of the kitchen clock, Rex wondered about John Calpin. Had Darrell Cruikshank done away with him, too? Had he heard about his research on his family and travelled halfway across the country to locate his mark in Glasgow? Calpin had been a child when Darrell was put away, so it couldn't have been a grudge killing.

From behind him, Rex heard Cruikshank call a number on his phone. "The other man, Malcolm Patterson, is not here," he stated.

"I don't know where is other man," the heavy Russian accent of an older male answered through the phone. "Find him." More words were spoken that Rex could not catch, but he felt weak with relief to hear Malcolm had not come to harm, at least not at the hands of the nephew or Ivan. Darrell Cruikshank confirmed something to the Russian and ended the call. "You were right," he told

Rex. "Car trouble. I always knew Jags were unreliable, but they're on their way. Never fear." He laughed unpleasantly.

"Answer me one thing," Rex said. "How did you get into your uncles' homes? They were sticklers for security and there was no sign of forced entry."

"They knew I was getting out and were expecting me any day. I'd sent word. They opened their door to me and faked a big welcome. Except Fred, who was taking his midday bath. When he didn't answer the bell, I climbed up a drainpipe to an open window round the back. He was a sitting duck! They'd got wind the Russians might be on to them. I showed more mercy than Ivan's gang would've. You heard what they did to the journalist?" The man snorted. "Just wait till you see what they'll do to you."

Rex's stomach performed a slow and sickening roll. He needed no convincing that Ivan the Terrible had earned his name if he had orchestrated John Calpin's death. Cruikshank spoke again.

"Ivan makes my lot look like fairy godmothers. All the same, I'm glad his cronies got to Calpin and his computer. I don't need any more family skeletons exposed and me going back inside."

"I suppose Ivan made you kill your old associates."

"It was an initiation, see? To prove myself."

Much as Rex appreciated getting answers as to who'd killed whom, it was cold comfort if he had to take the information with him to the grave. And what of Malcolm? With any luck, the Russians would turn up before he got home—if Ivan's son had not already taken him.

"And how long has your outfit been spying on me?"

"Long enough." Cruikshank came round to the table and leant against it, facing Rex, the knife held towards his hostage's throat. "We have an informant here keeping an eye on things."

"And who might that be?"

Cruikshank gave a sinister smirk. "You ask far too many questions, Mr. Graves. You know what happens to people who snoop." He touched the tip of the knife to Rex's lips. Rex's mouth went dry. "Like I said, you should've left well alone. Ivan Dragunov is extremely thorough in his elimination of people he don't trust."

Cold fear rippled down Rex's spine. He was planning to leap up and risk trying to overpower Cruikshank when he heard the faint but unmistakable sound of police sirens approaching.

Cruikshank tensed, his face hardened. "How can I get out of here?" He stuck the knifepoint into Rex's throat. "Tell me!"

"Try the river behind the house," Rex gasped. Desperate to be rid of the man, he added, "Beyond by the green is a path to a farm, which will take you to a road on the far side."

Cruickshank wrung open the back door and bolted into the garden. Rex touched his neck and felt blood. He snatched up a napkin from the table and ran through the house to the front door. He tore down the driveway and waved down the two patrol cars entering the cul-de-sac.

"I just had a man detain me at knife point," he told the first officer to descend from his vehicle. "He ran that way, towards the farm on the far side of the river." He pointed the uniformed policemen in the direction. "He's responsible for the four murders here in Notting Hamlet. He works for the MIR gang." Rex realized the first officer was regarding him with some scepticism.

"And you are?"

"Rex Graves, QC." He handed over his card, anxiously gazing in the direction Cruikshank had taken off in, just moments before.

The officer waved the other three uniformed men toward the river, yelling after them, "Suspect is on foot, armed with a knife. Be quick about it, lads."

"They'd better be quick," Rex told him. "A pair of German shepherds will likely maul him to bits if the farmer doesn't shoot him first." At least the boy, Alex, would still be at school and out of danger if Cruikshank managed to evade both the dogs and the shotgun.

"I'll dispatch a unit to Country Farm Road to cut him off, if he gets that far." The officer issued directions into his shoulder mic.

"The gangland boss is due here any moment with his bodyguard-chauffeur. They followed me from Luton in a black Jaguar, but it was too far away for me to get the number plate." After sitting at the kitchen table for what had seemed like an eternity, everything now appeared to be happening very fast. He felt light-headed.

"Are you all right, sir?" the officer asked, looking at Rex's hand holding the napkin to his throat.

"It's just a nick."

"Best get it seen to, all the same."

"My friend Malcolm Patterson, the owner of the house, is missing. We need to find him."

"We have your friend at the station."

"You do?" Rex supposed that was good news, at least better than the fate his imagination had concocted for Malcolm.

"He's in a bit of bother. Perhaps you can come and help clarify a couple of things."

At that moment, a man emerged from behind the house and waved. "And this must be the individual who rescued you from a potentially fatal situation," the officer said. Rex must have shown his confusion. "He called in the incident," the policeman explained.

The person in question approached with a swagger in his step. "Randall Gomez of Owl Lane, owner of Good-as-New Home Maintenance," he announced to the officer. "I hid in the shed until I was sure the coast was clear. Dangerous-looking bloke, yeah?" he said, addressing Rex. "Sorry I left you to fend for yourself. I thought if I burst in the kitchen, he might attack you right off. One stab and you'd've been a goner, mate. So I decided to wait for the cavalry."

Rex thanked him and shook his hand, though he privately questioned the man's retreat to the shed when his life had been in mortal danger. "But how did you know what was going on?" he asked as the officer stepped away to answer a call on his radio.

"I saw the old Vauxhall parked up the street. I'd seen it the day Valerie was murdered, but I couldn't tell the fuzz 'cause I was supposed to be visiting me mum the whole day. I just got this feeling, like. I was on my way to call on Mr. Patterson about the estimate for his kitchen when I saw the bloke slip into the house, looking about him all suspicious-like. He didn't see me. I'd parked short of the driveway and I ducked. Five minutes later, you drove past and I watched you go inside. I thought I'd better take a gander and went round the back. I saw him through the kitchen window with a knife to your neck and called nine-nine-nine."

Rex placed a hand on Randall's shoulder, the full extent of his relief washing over him. "The police arrived in the nick of time." Presumably, Ivan and his driver had seen the squad cars and turned back.

"You might've ended up dead like Ernest and Barry, and all," Gomez said, his chest puffed out over his beer belly. "We don't need another murder around here. I'm that chuffed I saved you. I'll be a local hero and get on the telly!"

The officer turned back and addressed them. "The fugitive has been apprehended and taken into custody. The dogs at the farm had him pinned down. He sustained an injury to his arm. I'll need a statement from you both."

"Any sign of the Jaguar?" Rex asked.

"I put out an APW."

"What Jaguar?" Gomez asked.

"This is a bigger story than either of us could ever have imagined," Rex told him. "It'll make national news. You'll be more than just a local hero."

And I could still end up dead, he thought.

TWENTY-THREE

GODMINTON STATION, AN OLD two-storey red-brick building that had served the local police force for almost a century, as indicated by a date-stone above the main entrance, did not appear to Rex to have changed much from the outside since its inception, and retained its small town character. The blue lamp provided a nightly warning to clients at the King's Head up the street not to get behind the wheel while under the influence and to generally behave in an orderly fashion.

Water stains on the drab green interior walls and a pervasive whiff of mildew attested to leaks in the old structure. A couple of constables milled about the premises while Rex waited to be taken in to see Malcolm after giving his statement. He occupied his time by reading through the draft chapters from John Calpin's book until the desk officer finally directed him to the first interview room down the hall, where Malcolm sat at a table with a severe-looking man sporting a rigid salt-and-pepper moustache.

"Chief Inspector," Rex greeted him with a brisk nod, having been notified of Cooper's presence by the desk officer.

"Did you cut yourself shaving?" Malcolm asked, spotting the sticking plaster on Rex's neck.

"No, Malcolm. A vicious gang member stuck a knife in my throat."

Rex had returned to the house briefly to dress his wound and to call Ken Penworth out of a meeting to warn him that his life was in danger.

Malcolm swallowed hard, his Adam's apple bobbing up and down. "Are you all right?" he gasped in dismay.

"Oh, aye. I just saw my life flash before my eyes." This was not far from the truth, but Rex tried to make light of the event for his friend's benefit. Malcolm, it appeared, had enough to worry about. "I understand you're in here for perverting the course of justice." Rex pulled up one of the stark chairs and took a seat opposite Detective Chief Inspector Cooper. "Where's your lawyer?" he asked his friend seated beside him at the metal table.

"I waived my right to one. I was waiting for you."

Rex curbed his exasperation. "I left you a message. Why didn't you call me?"

"I did. You didn't answer."

"That must have been after Cruikshank took my phone. Hopefully I'll get it back unless he tossed it."

"Cruikshank?" Malcolm asked in surprise.

"Darrell. He murdered his four old associates in Notting Hamlet, but he didn't kill John Calpin. The MIR gang have that dubious honour."

"Mr. Patterson has been telling me about this John Calpin and the MIR gang," the detective intervened. "Quite honestly, I thought it was a load of bollocks. But I just got through a quick interview with your assailant and it seems he and his Russian friends are all in it together, and an Ivan Dragunov ordered the hit on the Cruikshank gang."

"But what about the word MIR daubed in blood on the victims' foreheads?" Malcolm asked Rex. "Why would Darrell Cruikshank have done that?"

"It's their signature," Rex said. "He was acting on behalf of the Russian mob, although I don't think it took much arm-twisting."

"I thought blood was thicker than water," his friend remarked.

"Not in this case. Darrell is bitter about the way his family hung him oot to dry. His uncles got off with far worse crimes than he was charged with. They had the best counsel money could buy. Darrell, on the other hand, was penalized for not helping the prosecution make a case against them. Something he now regrets."

"This time around," the detective put in, "he's prepared to give up Ivan and his gang, even though he'll never be a free man again. The most he can expect are prison privileges."

Rex showed DCI Cooper a page from his notebook. "This is what Mr. Patterson inadvertently rubbed off when administering to the victims, the Russian gangland symbol, МИР."

"Not that inadvertently. That the letters shown here and described by Mr. Patterson constitute his initials did not escape my attention in spite of the back-to-front N."

"Did you make the Russian connection?" Rex asked.

"We might have if we'd had the benefit of this vital piece of information from the start," the inspector fumed.

"Surely Cruikshank's confession exonerates me," Malcolm said to the detective.

Cooper regarded him with a jaundiced eye. "Not from tampering with evidence. That's a very serious offense, Mr. Patterson. You, of all people, with your background in forensic pathology, should know that."

"Yes," Malcolm said, slumping his shoulders, contrite as could be.

"We found traces of the letters," the detective informed Rex. "But not enough to be distinguishable. Your friend here is looking at up to ten years in prison."

"I know," Rex said with an apologetic grimace. "If I were his lawyer, I'd plead emotional stress and utter stupidity. If you need further evidence of who was involved, I have it here." He brandished a stapled sheaf of paper from his briefcase.

"What's that?" Malcolm asked.

"It's from Calpin's manuscript detailing how 'Fred the Spanner' Forspaniak bombed the Dragunovs' car, killing four of Ivan's close family members, and how Ivan vowed retribution. Calpin led him to his enemies' hiding place, and Ivan orchestrated the hit on the enforcer and the other three victims after waiting twenty years for revenge. The journalist sealed his own fate at the same time. This other chapter details MIR methodology, including the stamping of their name in blood on their victims. Almost to my detriment, I unwittingly lured Darrell Cruikshank back to Notting Hamlet. Now we have the whole picture." And how satisfying that was, Rex thought.

"Am I free to go?" Malcolm asked the detective wearily. "I've been here over two hours."

"I could keep you a lot longer before I have to charge you. And charge you I should." Cooper stroked a tip of his moustache in quick succession. A brief pause. "Fine. You can go, for now, but don't leave the country."

Rex bid the detective a cordial goodbye. "Mr. Patterson has not been himself since his wife's death," he uttered under his breath after Malcolm had left the interview room. "I think the murders in his community triggered his stress and anxiety and caused him to behave irrationally."

"And, granted, he did come to me with a full confession," the detective acknowledged. "I'll do what I can. No guarantees. Thank you for your assistance in this case. The Bedfordshire Police are profoundly grateful."

"Thank Malcolm. He brought me down here."

Rex found his friend in the lobby. "Pub?" he suggested.

"Thought you'd never ask. I could murder a pint. It's no fun being on the other side of the law. Do you think Cooper will press charges?"

"If he does, I'm hoping he'll make a case for leniency."

On the walk to the King's Head, Rex filled Malcolm in on the details of his ordeal at the house.

"I can't tell you how sorry I am, Rex. I shouldn't have dragged you into this in the first place."

"I'm glad you did. Truly." So long as the rest of the Dragunov gang were caught.

"Is the house a mess?" Malcolm asked.

"Just your study. Someone knocked over your cup of tea and ruined your editions of *The Lancet*."

"That was me. I heard a loud, ominous rap at the door and panicked. I knew it couldn't be good."

"You're lucky it was the police and not Darrell Cruikshank. The Russians were on their way. Hopefully, they'll be apprehended before they can carve anyone else up."

"Poor John Calpin. He got too close to the truth." Malcolm gave an agonized sigh. "Let's eat at the pub. I don't fancy going home just yet. What if Stroganoff and his gang are waiting for us there?"

"Dragunov, Malcolm. By the way, it seems they have a local informant."

"I know. DCI Cooper told me."

The two men paused for a gap in the traffic before crossing the road to the thatch-roofed pub. Rex couldn't wait for his pint.

"I thought at first of the Leontiev family across the river, but Cruikshank said within the community. I'm thinking Mr. Woods on Fox Lane."

"The chem teacher who poisoned the dog?" Malcolm shook his head.

"We don't know for certain that he did. But if he was spying on the residents, he wouldn't have wanted it yapping away every time he left his house, especially at night."

"I've seen him walking about Notting Hamlet, but he rarely speaks to anybody," Malcolm said as a patron opened the door to the King's Head, releasing a waft of beery fumes.

Rex followed his friend to an isolated booth. "If he's oot of a job, he may have been tempted by a bribe from the Russians until he can sell his house."

"Stands to reason. But you're wrong."

"How do you mean?" Rex asked in surprise.

"Lottie Green is the informant, according to Cooper, who presumably got it from Darrell Cruikshank."

"Our Lottie? Your cleaning lady?"

"The same. The busybody who is always on some neighbourly errand and who knows everything that goes on in the Hamlet. Who better? She knew what we were up to, and what happens? The Russian mob turns up on my doorstep. Lottie apparently succumbed to pressure or some form of compensation. Or perhaps she fancied herself as a double agent."

"She did a good job," Rex said in a constrained voice, wondering how he would ever be able to trust an old biddy again.

Malcolm waved to the young female server from their previous visit. Rex ordered a Guinness and Malcolm a pint of bitter, and they decided on the fish and chips. Rex decided he deserved a bit of stodge after all he had been through that day. Lottie's perfidy was harder to digest. He preferred to assume she had not known about the Russians' involvement when she saw Ernest lying under the piano. But had she been spying on the old man? She couldn't have realized what she was getting herself into, otherwise she would never have told him about the BMW, Rex reasoned. At least her gossip regarding that and the name Frankie had been reliable and had set him on the right course.

"When the residents discover the murders were a mob killing and not random—a bunch of criminals getting their just desserts—they'll feel safer," he told Malcolm. "Hopefully the properties will start selling. And now that the publicity has put Notting Hamlet on the map, perhaps the signposts will be restored."

"I expect it was vandals, or else the Cruikshank gang seeking anonymity. At least you got rid of one undesirable element in the neighbourhood. Wish you could get rid of the bikers."

Their drinks arrived, and the two men attacked them.

"No place is perfect, Malcolm. Are you going to call on Charlotte? Perhaps flowers this time?"

"Why not? I can bring her up to speed." Malcolm put his head in his hands and groaned. "I'll be so glad when this is all over."

"Me too," Rex said, thinking he'd be relieved to get home safe and sound.

TWENTY-FOUR

A WEEK LATER, REX sat in his chambers in Edinburgh during a tea break, reading a newspaper. The arrest of the prominent members of the MIR Gang had made national headline news. Ivan Dragunov's enterprises in East London and Essex had been raided and found to front activities ranging from protection rackets and wholesale distribution of recreational drugs to prostitution and human trafficking. The members were now awaiting trial. Darrell Cruikshank was awaiting sentencing.

The media gave the Bedfordshire Police glowing reviews for wrapping up the five related murders. Randall Gomez, exploiting his fifteen minutes of fame, had recounted his tale of heroism to any reporter who would listen, and listen they did. He told them he'd almost sold Kev Cruikshank his timeshare in Spain. Rex's part in cracking the case was made public knowledge, and his phones had not stopped ringing. It had been a long week.

Helen was flying home with Julie that day after completing their cruise to Gran Turk, the Dominican Republic, Curaçao, and Orangestad in Aruba. His fiancée's text messages had described alternately lush and rocky islands, colourful Dutch architecture and wedding cake mansions, tree monkeys and exotic birds, Caribbean beaches and glitzy marinas. It all seemed so far away and unreal.

No doubt Helen would say the same of his adventure. And, hopefully, forgive him for not going on the cruise. Rex smiled in eager anticipation of taking the train down to Derby on Friday to see her and enjoy a weekend without mobsters or murder.

ABOUT THE AUTHOR

Born in Bloomington, Indiana, and now living in Florida, C. S. Challinor was educated in Scotland and England, and holds a joint honors degree in Latin and French from the University of Kent, Canterbury, as well as a diploma in Russian from the Pushkin Institute in Moscow.